EXHIBITS
AN ANTHOLOGY BY 67 PRESS

67 Press
Winston Salem, North Carolina

This book is a work of fiction. Names, characters, places
and incidents either are products of the authors' imagination
or are used fictitiously. Any resemblance to actual events or
locales or persons living or dead is entirely coincidental.

Death Pitch by Mike Sherer first appeared in the Spring 2016 York Literary Review.
Dummy by Douglas Milliken was previously published by The Manchester Review

Cover Design by Matt Ankerson
Cover Layout by Bradley Powell
Cover images "Girl with Balloon" and "Greetings from Dad" by Oliva LaVack

ISBN: 978-0-9966616-2-1
All rights reserved including the right of reproduction
in whole or in part in any form.
Manufactured in the United States

TABLE OF CONTENTS

We dedicate this book to the following people we lost in 2016 who continue to have a monumental influence on us –

Alan Rickman, Clarence Reid, George Martin, Phife Dawg, Ken Howard, Merle Haggard, Pearl Washington, Gordie Howe, Ralph Stanley, Jim Harrison, Alan Vega, Mr. Fuji, Gene Wilder, W.P. Kinsella, Bill Nunn, Arnold Palmer, Eddie Harsch, Leonard Cohen, Leon Russell, Harper Lee, Prince, Muhammed Ali, and David Bowie.

EXHIBITS
AN INTRODUCTION

Thank you for purchasing Exhibits, the third anthology of short stories from 67 Press.

It's an eclectic group of characters featuring drug addicts, Gods and fallen rock stars inhabiting the same space. There's bedbugs, S&M, and a shape shifting dinosaur. There's excess and poverty, love and hate, and a well-meaning apocalypse for good measure.

If you've read the Salmagundi and Affinity (shame on you if you haven't!) you're going to see elements of both in Exhibits. I believe we've captured the raw unbridled state of the Salmagundi and paired it with the reflectiveness of Affinity which allows Exhibits to have both experimentalism and accessibility. I look at it like the third album from your favorite indie band. The one where they finally brought it all together but hadn't sold out yet. What more could you ask for?

Though it's a disparate group of stories, they are all parts of the great human drama we live every day. Their insecurities, guilt and fears are our own magnified by their circumstances. Most of us live lives of quiet desperation, happy to make it through another day still breathing. These story tellers and their tales do not, they put every intense surreal moment out on display for all of us to see.

Thanks again, we're glad to have you be a part of the show.

Alan Wright
67 Press

EXHIBITS

THE OTHER SIDE OF THE CAGE
LEAH MUELLER

The Audubon Zoo on Ash Wednesday is an eerily tranquil place. Ed and I decided to take advantage of the stillness and slip through one of the side gates without paying admission. An hour earlier, we'd each swallowed two hits of acid, and the effects were coming on strong. We swooped through the gate as though a sudden updraft had caught our bodies and rendered us helpless. Probably we would have gotten away with our minor act of theft, but I giggled inadvertently, and the ticket vendor spotted us. "Um, excuse me" she said. "Aren't you forgetting something?"

I gaped in terror at the direction of the voice. A portly, middle-aged black woman stared serenely back at me from the tiny fee window. In an infinitely patient tone, she explained, "Both of you can go into the zoo for free. I just didn't want you to walk past me without saying hello."

I was astonished by her lack of anger. The zoo normally cost ten bucks, and we only had fifty dollars of our face painting money left. Ed had spent most of his proceeds on

Bourbon Street for cups of warm, overpriced beer, and we'd blown the rest of our modest wad on food and lodging.

The two of us had arrived in New Orleans four days earlier, nearly penniless after scraping together our funds in Madison, and then hitting the road in my mother's pickup truck. My mother lived in San Miguel de Allende. For reasons unbeknownst to me, the Mexican government had forbidden her to keep her beloved truck in the country, and she had reluctantly given it to me as a gift. I hadn't bothered with the necessary title paperwork, and the license tabs had expired. I wasn't worried, since the cops never pulled me over, even though Ed and I couldn't have been more conspicuous as we barreled down Interstate 57 in a pickup truck with expired Texas plates. At the beginning of our journey, the cab of the truck was filled almost to overflowing with dirty Wisconsin snowdrifts. I'd shoved bottles of white wine into the snow so we could enjoy chilled beverages at our pit stops. Originally, this had worked brilliantly, but the snow had completely melted by the time we reached Mississippi, and we'd also run out of wine.

I grinned stupidly at the ticket vendor, and she smiled back. "That's what I'm talking about," she said. "Enjoy the zoo. It certainly is a lovely afternoon."

We waved at her merrily and continued on our way. The late afternoon sunshine was already waning, and cool breezes blew through the magnolia trees. The puffs of wind seemed to increase and decrease randomly, as if someone were turning on a giant air blower and then abruptly shutting it off. Ed and I sailed along like boats, catching the random wind gusts, twirling in circles with our arms outstretched.

"This is good acid," Ed commented. "I'm glad that guy in the dorm was so generous with us. We certainly didn't deserve it."

Four nights earlier, after we'd arrived in New Orleans with only twenty dollars in our pockets, Ed and I had driven to the campus of Tulane University. Ed had fallen into discussion with a privileged young Deadhead who'd proclaimed, "You two are living the life! You're the coolest people EVER!" and offered us the use of his single bed. Ed and I had squashed our bodies together on the narrow mattress, while our new friend had slept on his linoleum floor. In the morning, the generous fellow had given us four hits of powerful acid and told us to enjoy Mardi Gras.

Though I'd had a fond vision of the two of us wandering through the streets of the Quarter on Fat Tuesday, ripped to the gills on LSD like Dennis Hopper and Peter Fonda in Easy Rider, I'd decided it was better to wait until the revelry was over. Mardi Gras was a drunken, crowded, sinister event, and our face painting efforts had abruptly turned ugly when a police horse slipped in a puddle of beer and capsized in front of us. Ed and I'd dodged the flying hooves, and the officer had flown through the air and landed face-down, on the pavement. Fortunately, our meager stash of face painting supplies was unscathed. We'd been able to resume our efforts only a few minutes later. Extracting money from drunks had been no problem, but saving our cash was impossible. Our original plan of returning to Madison with hundreds of dollars was obviously not going to pan out.

Anxiety about our future was the furthest thing from our minds as we skipped along the sidewalk past the lion cages, with their pacing felines (one of whom roared comically as we strolled by, causing us to shriek with laughter), the primate house with its earthy smell of simian urine, and the outdoor dolphin pool. Ed paused for a while in front of the pool, and said, "It's hot. I think I'll go for a swim!"

several times, until people gaped openly at him, and I finally pulled him away.

After an hour of this, we collapsed onto an iron bench. A strong breeze pushed through the heavy magnolia trees and hit us both in the face. Ed flinched slightly. He was prone to flinching, an after-effect of having spent his first eighteen years dodging sudden blows from his father. I'd once seen a childhood picture of Ed and his family. He and the other family members had assembled in front of their split-level Wisconsin home. The females had looked humorless and bored, the men menacing in the pedestrian manner that was typical of the mid-1960s. Ed's father had cropped hair, rolled-up white shirt sleeves, and the requisite mouth-dangling cigarette. He'd looked exactly like the sort of guy who would hit a kid for no reason.

Seven-year-old Ed had been standing to the left of his slightly older, more confident brother. Chuck had gazed arrogantly into the camera, but Ed hovered on the edge of the group and clutched his face with both hands. Ed's shirt had escaped from the inside of his dress pants, and the two bottom buttons were undone. Obviously, Ed was in a state of disrepair, but the other family members were completely oblivious to the source of his unhappiness, and not a bit interested in resolution.

The February sun sank lower, and the zoo became quiet, as if all the animals had decided to rest simultaneously. People filed past us, then gradually disappeared without so much as a glance in our direction. A dozen stray peacocks strutted in front of our bench in a slow-motion parade. Suddenly, one at a time, each of the birds flapped its iridescent wings and ascended to the top branches of the magnolia trees. They snuggled their bodies into the white and pink blossoms, tucked their heads under their wings, and fell asleep.

Ed and I gaped at the scene, unable to believe our eyes. "Do you think this would look as beautiful if we weren't tripping?" Ed whispered.

"I don't know," I replied. "I think it would probably be just as beautiful, but we wouldn't notice it as much."

This made perfect sense to Ed, and he nodded with apparent delight. "You're right," he said. His voice sounded unnaturally loud, like he was speaking through a microphone. Ed leaned backward and pushed his spine into the iron slats of the park bench. He rested for a second, but then his eyes widened, as if remembering something that he had deliberately forgotten.

The color drained abruptly from Ed's face, and purple blotches appeared on his pale cheeks. The remaining white portions appeared translucent, and I could see dark veins and corpuscles underneath the surface of his skin. Ed's expression slowly changed to one of abject terror. "We have to return home tomorrow!" he announced. "The wind chill in Madison is going to be below zero, and I don't have a place to live."

I was seized with pity for him, and an accompanying to desire to help, but then I remembered that I didn't have a home, either. After only a few months of cohabitation, my boyfriend Steve and I had recently decided to go our separate ways. Apartment hunting in freezing temperatures was always tricky, especially without deposit money or steady employment. I'd managed to score a part time job as a driver for Badger Cab, but few shifts were available. To make matters worse, I had an extremely poor sense of direction. Ed had obligingly accompanied me on most of my driving assignments. He possessed an extensive knowledge of the city's layout, gleaned from many months of aimless meandering.

A few weeks earlier, I'd informed my roommates that Ed would be crashing in the living room for an indefinite period, and there was nothing they could do about it. No one had argued with me about this, not even my boyfriend. While Steve had slumbered peacefully upstairs during the beginning of my pre-dawn taxi shifts, Ed had risen from his reclining position on the couch and met me at the front door, tattered map in hand. He'd never shirked this voluntary task, or hesitated for even a moment. We called our ritual "going cabbing" and it was always the high point of an otherwise hellish week.

After a few moderately lucrative cab shifts, I had managed to save enough money for our escape to New Orleans. My eviction from the house had meant that Ed was displaced from the couch as well. It'd made sense for the two of us to flee south together. My housemates had all felt sorry for Steve and thought that he was the injured party, but now at least Steve had a roof over his head, a set of tuition-paying parents, and a future in corporate America. Ed's complete lack of such advantages was the reason for our close bond, the source of our mutual attraction. He and I were card-carrying members of the Loser tribe, and we needed to stick together and shelter each other against the onslaughts of stronger, more rapacious clans.

I opened my mouth to tell him this, but it was too late. Ed was weeping copiously, without making a sound. Globs of water coursed down his cheeks, blurring the purple splotches until his face resembled a watercolor painting. Ed's tears dripped onto the ribbed collar of his tee-shirt, completely drenching the fabric. He lowered his head, shook it back and forth in a gesture of futility. "I don't understand" he sobbed. "Everyone always tells me to just find a job and keep going to it, and then everything will be okay. I've never had a job that didn't suck shit, and I don't think I ever will."

I couldn't fathom the degree of self-loathing that would make a twenty-three-year-old man decide that his employment options would be miserable for the rest of his life. Despite my own hardships, I remained firmly entrenched in the belief that my luck would change, that my current limitations were caused by a combination of youth and poor time management. Reality had repeatedly failed to confirm my optimism, and yet I was remarkably stubborn in my commitment to it. I smiled at Ed and placed one of my hands on his shoulder, but I could think of nothing to say.

Ed cried hard for several more minutes, and then subsided. He shook his head again, and a few stray tears flew around him like droplets from a hose. "I'm sorry," he said.

"It's all right," I assured him. "Life's not for the squeamish."

Ed mopped his face with the palm of one of his hands. He squinted at me through his tear-drenched eyelashes, and then suddenly smiled. "Well, at least the winter is half over."

I realized that the sky had grown completely dark. The early evening air was cool, but pleasant. I could hear the peacocks rustling fitfully in the trees in search of better sleeping positions. There were no other sounds except for the distant buzzing of insects. The zoo grounds were completely devoid of other humans. "I wonder what time this place closes?" Ed asked. "Did you happen to notice the hours while we were sneaking inside?"

Both of us laughed then, relieved that we were able to find humor in our self-imposed ordeal, our mutual idiocy. "I forgot to look at the sign," I said. "I was trying to be invisible, so I didn't see anything."

"I guess we'd better go," Ed replied uncertainly. He rose to his feet, lifted his filthy, shredded backpack from the ground, and hoisted it over one shoulder. His eyes darted back and forth, then rested on mine. "Do you happen to remember which way we came in?" he asked.

At that moment, I realized how dependent I was upon Ed's sense of direction, his usually unfailing ability to navigate the two of us out of any geographical predicament. I had simply followed him into the zoo, assuming that he would remember the route to the gate when it was time to leave. The zoo was spacious and beautifully landscaped, with groves of trees that stretched away from us in all directions. In the darkness, the groves appeared sinister and maze-like.

The two of us stumbled away from the park bench. "I guess this way is as good as any," Ed said, pointing towards the closest blob of trees. Bravely, we forged ahead past scores of darkened cages. Occasionally, a slumbering animal stirred as we passed its cage. A Bengal tiger lifted his head and peered at us irritably, then decided that we weren't worth his time and went back to sleep. The tiger was comfortable in his cage; he knew where he fit. On the other hand, Ed and I were searching for a niche that existed somewhere outside the scope of our knowledge. We were on the other side of the cage, but we were utterly clueless.

After a while, we realized that we were navigating in circles. We passed the tiger again, but this time he did not even stir. I felt strangely tranquil, as if it didn't matter if we ever left the zoo grounds. "We keep ending up in the same place," Ed announced. He leaned casually against a railing and stared at me with an odd smile on his face. Since his earlier meltdown, Ed had achieved a state of Zen calm. "Perhaps there's someone around that we could ask."

As soon as the words were out of his mouth, I noticed an elderly man on a bicycle. He wobbled towards us deliberately, then finally came to a halt about six feet away. The man wore a navy blue uniform shirt, which bore a plastic name tag that identified him as a zoo employee. "The zoo's closed," he said unnecessarily. He gestured expansively towards the right, but I could see nothing, except for darkness. "The exit's over there. You can't possibly miss it." He climbed back onto his bicycle and laboriously pedaled away.

Ed and I pressed on toward the exit, but it remained hidden. "You know, this is a beautiful place for a person to be lost," Ed said. His face grew thoughtful, and he smiled. "That woman at the front gate was a saint. She just wanted to make sure we acknowledged her humanity. She didn't even want our money."

I nodded vigorously, and was immediately lost in my own rabbit hole of thought. The two of us had no reason to rush to the exit. Eventually, we would find the gate, and then the adjacent park trails would lead us inexorably towards St. Charles Avenue. My mother's truck sat beside the streetcar tracks, patiently awaiting our arrival. Once we found the vehicle, we would return to our cheap motel room, sleep for a few hours, and drive back to Madison with a few dollars in our pockets. Despite our ill luck, people had been kind to us, as they so often were.

Struck by the absurdity of our ordeal, I began to laugh uncontrollably. After a sidelong glance and a moment of bewilderment, Ed joined me. Soon, the two of us were guffawing loudly, joyfully, holding our sides, wiping tears from our eyes. "Lost in the zoo," Ed gasped. "Only you and I would get ourselves into such a predicament."

Suddenly, out of nowhere, the elderly zoo guard reappeared. He seemed to be in no particular hurry to hasten our departure. The guard pedaled our way on his bicycle, parked in front of us, and smiled. "You sure like our zoo, don't you?" he chuckled. We laughed even harder, and he pointed again, this time towards the left. There, in plain sight, was the exit turnstile. Beyond the gate, the park grounds stretched out expansively in all directions.

We thanked him profusely and pushed our way through the turnstile towards freedom. The metal grates clanked behind us as we made our way into the park. I grasped Ed's hand and gave it a little squeeze, looked into his eyes, and smiled. Ed smiled back, and then we continued our long walk towards my waiting vehicle, and the road ahead.

CHUTES AND LADDERS
EMILY AUMAN

"I kind of think he sucks. Is that bad?" George chuckled a little as he said this, taking a puff from his newly lit Parliament.

"I don't really think opinions can be mean. Probably shouldn't say it to his face, but it's okay to not like his stuff. I don't like it either. Edgy doesn't always mean interesting, you know? Like none of his stuff makes me think at all." I don't smoke, but sometimes I sit outside with George while he does. We take the opportunity to talk about the deep stuff or sit in silence or complain about fellow "writers" who make us feel better about ourselves.

"I told all of my coworkers we're sleeping together," he says, smirking. I laugh out loud.

"They fall for it?"

"They congratulated me." I smile and take a sip of my beer, looking out at the open air. Now that it's cold, you don't have the frogs and crickets filling the silence, but that's okay with us.

I first met George six years ago at the pizza place we both worked. I was the girl in charge of screaming a greeting at people when they walked in the door, making salads, and flirting with the manager despite my jailbait status. The last part wasn't in the job description, but you know that clause in all job descriptions that says "and whatever else management sees fit?" Well, management saw my big blue eyes fit for their entertainment. George was a cook. He stood silently and assembled pizzas over and over again. Flatten crust, dock crust, sauce, cheese, toppings ("but not too many—we're not made of money"). His unlisted task was listening to the methamphetamine-induced conversations of the women in charge of making dough. They would talk about the smutty books they'd read and gossip about other people who worked there and then he would tell me about it. We'd lean against our cars after we got off of work and talk about music or how much our franchisee's wife hated him.

It was pure coincidence that we were both writers and something we only realized about each other a couple years into our friendship. George likes to write shocking comedy: Jurassic Park fan fiction with roller skates or futuristic humanoids all suffering from sex addiction. He is good, both in conversation and in writing, at making you laugh and contemplate at the same time. Sometimes, if he's feeling serious and he's read too much Tolkien, he writes about his times in Philadelphia, where he spent a year experiencing everything but brotherly love. I write about sad stuff mostly. I write the dramatization of feelings I have vaguely experienced. While neither of us has changed the world, we are, admittedly, overly-critical of others who claim to have the art down.

"Back to Joe. Doesn't he realize that having a character obsessively snort cocaine is not a new concept? Bret Easton Ellis did it, but he did it *well*." George goes through a Bret Easton Ellis phase once a year or so (I say he's been stung by a BEE).

"Right? People are not one-dimensional and just because you make them flawed in such a visible way doesn't make them less superficial, and a superficial protagonist is exhausting for everyone." He nods and pulls one last drag out of his cigarette. The blanket I brought outside isn't making up for the brisk November wind, but I still don't want to go inside.

"Playground?"

"Sure. Let me grab another." He grabs and shakes the empty beer bottle resting on the brick awning under my mother's large picture window. "You want one?" I nod affirmatively. I get up and place the blanket on the bench I just vacated, wrapping my coat around me tightly to combat the chill.

We walk in silence under the synthetic glow of my neighborhood's streetlights. It's just after 1 A.M., according to my phone, and the houses once littered with my adolescent vandalism are all dark. Subdivisions are a good place to grow up because everyone knows you by sight, but very few people actually bother knowing your name. It's a good balance of neighborliness and cooperation. At the end of the main road sits a Baptist church, modest in literal size and congregation size for a church in the Bible Belt. I'd learned to ride my bike in its parking lot while they were having a wedding. I asked the groom first. He said it was okay. Maybe it turned into a good story for them. "You know, during our wedding ceremony a little blonde girl was riding her bike sans training wheels between the cars in the parking lot."

Behind the church, at the bottom of a hill, was a reasonably maintained playground. Late at night I often went to it and would swing on their big swings, looking up at the stars and meditating about life. When I would do this as a kid I would cautiously watch the graveyard next to it, making sure no visitors rose from the dead. I started bringing people with me when I was a teenager and had my first kiss in the gazebo by the playground's entrance. George comes with me a lot, although he doesn't actually swing. He plants himself firmly into the seat, his knees at an awkward ninety degrees, and fidgets with the chains on each side of his torso.

"I should write a story where playground equipment turns into monsters and starts attacking the children," he said soberly.

"I had a dream like that once."

"Can you imagine?" he giggled, "Just a red plastic slide with teeth eating kids as they slid down..." He can't continue, he's laughing too hard. "How ridiculous would that be?" I pull hard on the second beer, visualizing the faded rocking horses tearing from their rusty springs and whinnying wildly.

"That's very Jim Henson of you."

"I promise all of the monsters will obsessively snort cocaine in between the feasting."

"Duh, at least then it'll be edgy."

THE GUN SHOW LOOPHOLE
ANDREW WHITE

I felt her eyes on me before I opened my own. My mother always had a sense of when my nights had gotten out of hand. A headache pounded at my temples. Somehow I needed to make it from this bed to the front door.

I rolled onto my side and opened my eyes to pillars of sunlight forcing their way through gaps in my blinds. Why people insisted on being awake during the day was beyond me. Mom was peeking through a crack in the door.

"Can I help you?" I said. She pushed the door open another few inches so her face was visible.

"Gabe is here," she said. What was he doing at my house? I thought.

"Alright. I'll be down in a second."

She hesitated as if there were something else she wanted to say, then walked back downstairs. It was getting old waking up to her staring at me. I knew she was just checking to make sure I was still breathing, but nothing made me more uncomfortable than when she watched me sleep.

I sat up and waited for the room to stop spinning. I realized I had slept in my clothes from the day before, sneakers included. My father's voice traveled up from the first floor. I wondered why he was home from work this early in the afternoon before I realized that it was Saturday. Whatever happened last night, I better not have driven.

My stomach lurched and I fought back the urge to vomit. All I had to do was get down the stairs and out of the door. I struggled to force myself to my feet. Whoever claimed that drug addicts don't have any willpower had never tried to wake up on a morning like this.

My laundry sat unwashed in a heap by my closet door. There was no point in changing into a different set of dirty clothes. Since I had been wearing the same five t-shirts and two pairs of jeans for a few weeks now, there was no guarantee that what I picked up was any cleaner than what I had on already. I didn't have anybody to impress with hygiene anyway. I patted my pockets. Phone? Wallet? Keys? Check. It was time to face the day.

I steadied myself on the banister and stumbled down the stairs. My coordination was still impaired from the previous night. I was dizzier than usual and my limbs were like lead weights. The buzz felt like some kind of muscle relaxer, or maybe a benzo, but I couldn't be sure.

When I was able to put the living room into focus, I saw both of my parents making cordial conversation with my closest friend, Gabe. He took his eyes from my father just long enough to shoot me a quick smile. Chances are he knew more about my night than I did.

"It's thoughtful of you to come pick Jamie up," my mother said.

"You know how he likes to oversleep," my father added.

"The cookout wouldn't be the same without him," Gabe said.

"You boys won't be doing any drinking, will you?" my mother asked.

"No ma'am," Gabe said "We just wanted to have a little send-off for Jamie and the other people heading off to college."

"What school did you decide on?" my father asked. "You'll be going in the fall as well, right?"

"No sir. I'll be working with my uncle. I plan to take a semester or two off to save up some money."

"That's exactly what I did after high school. It never hurts to have some extra time to prepare," my mother said, looking at me as if to say, "See! This is how a young man is supposed to behave!"

"You ready to go, Gabe?" I asked.

"I'm ready when you are," he said. "Thank you for the tea, Mrs. Gibson."

"You're welcome, Gabe. You boys enjoy yourself."

My parents stood to walk us out. When the front door was safely shut behind us and we were out of earshot, I turned to Gabe.

"A cookout? Really?"

"What was I supposed to tell them?"

"If you stopped showing up before I was out of bed, you wouldn't have to tell them anything," I said, hopping in the passenger seat of Gabe's truck.

I looked around as we left the neighborhood, but my Civic was missing. "Do you know where my car is?"

"It's where you left it last night. You remember, don't you?"

"Funny. Seriously, where's my car?"

"You don't remember last night at all?" Gabe asked.

"Was it really that memorable?"

"Fair enough." Gabe crinkled his nose and cracked the windows. "You stink, dude."

"Sorry, my ride showed up before I had the chance to shower."

"Whoever it was should have known you'd be sleeping. What kind of maniac is awake at this hour?" Gabe said sarcastically, pointing at the digital clock on his dashboard. It read 3:36 P.M. He started the car and pulled around to leave the cul-de-sac. "You've got the money right?"

"Shit! We're missing the gun show!" I said, reaching for my wallet and leafing through it to make sure I had woken up with the cash. Thankfully, it was still there. This wouldn't have been the first time I had an empty wallet after a blackout.

"That's where we're going. Why else would I come scoop you?" he said.

"To enjoy my company?"

Gabe chuckled. A few minutes later we were pulling up in front of Newt's house. My car was parked on the street out front and appeared to be in one piece. Our buddy Todd sat on the curb shouting into his phone. He thrust his finger at the ground and scowled. Then, seeing us, he gave a wave and smile. Gabe parked the truck on the street opposite my Civic and we hopped out.

"I'll drive," I said, taking the keys from my pocket.

"You sure you're good to drive?"

I ignored him. Gun shows at the Richmond showplace were a rare treat. Though I had no interest in guns themselves, they were a profitable means to an end. Whenever gun shows came to our city, Gabe, Toddler, and I were always sure to make a pit stop.

Reaching into my back pocket, I took out a fold of cash and handed it to Gabe in the back seat of my Honda. Under normal circumstances, handing money over to anyone without drugs for sale was against my code of ethics. It just didn't make sense wasting hard-earned cash on something I could just as easily steal.

Handing money over to Gabe was an exception. For a junky, he maintained a shockingly clean-cut appearance. His consistent haircut, collared shirt, and polite manner made it hard to believe he had a drug problem. He would have looked more at home with a briefcase instead of a needle in his hand. These qualities made him ideal for handling the purchase.

Years spent at the shooting range with his father and seasons on his high school rifle team had given him the ability to set the NRA-worshiping gun dealers at ease. As much as I hated letting my money out of sight, right now there was no better place for it than Gabe's pocket. Toddler hung his phone up and climbed in the back seat.

"God damn coke heads. I hate fucking coke heads," he said, pocketing his phone.

"Everything alright?" I asked.

"I should be asking you, buddy," he said with a grin. "I'm surprised you made it home last night."

After a short drive, we made it to the gun show parking lot. Gabe exited the car, being careful not to scratch the paint on the fire-engine-red F150 in the spot next to us. He strode off towards the entrance, leaving Toddler and I feeling decidedly out of place.

There was no room in my heart or wallet for anything other than opiates and booze, but high school provided an insatiable market for pot, ecstasy, mushrooms, pills, and every other soft drug I could source. The cash I had passed off to Gabe had been earned breaking down a few sheets of acid into strips and single hits. An afternoon's pushing would bring in the same amount of money as a two-week paycheck at any place that hired eighteen-year-olds without work experience.

Since his twenty-first birthday, Gabe had made three trips to purchase handguns with Toddler and me. He wouldn't admit it, but I think he liked buying the guns more than the money they provided. I was all about the end game. It took Toddler to put it all together. This scam was his brainchild. You could look down on him all you wanted, but in my opinion, he'd earned a certain degree of respect for his creativity.

Todd "Toddler" Lerner had recently turned eighteen, though you wouldn't know it by looking at him. His small stature and boyish appearance made him look half his age, earning him his moniker. Unlike Gabe, Toddler was clearly a drug addict. He was gaunt and pale with an unhealthy look about him. His hazel eyes twitched around deep purple pits in his skull, darting from place to place as if focused on a fly only he could see.

Toddler was simultaneously the most likely of my friends to steal my wallet and the best hustling partner I knew. He was fiercely opportunistic and devoid of any semblance of moral compass. As long as you understood his ethical retardation, he was predictable and not unpleasant to be around.

Out of all of us, Toddler had to be the biggest disappointment to his family, and that was saying something. His father was in the scrap metal business and had worked his way up from a single pickup truck to owning several scrap yards that sold mass quantities of assorted metals to corporate buyers overseas. Toddler had inherited his father's business acumen and used it liberally in the worst possible ways. He had worked for his father weighing metal and cutting checks for a number of years before he was caught writing out checks to friends for metal they didn't bring in.

No amount of private schooling could rein in his innate tendency to break rules. He once told me an expensive shrink his parents made him see had decided he was an "oppositional defiant." He took pride in the label. Any authority figure, regardless of setting, was received with scorn and misbehavior. Had he applied himself in a productive way, there was no doubt in my mind that he would have been a self-reliant adult. As things stood, he was a high school dropout who hadn't worked a legitimate job a day in his life.

"What do you think he'll pick up this time?" Toddler asked. I shrugged. Gabe knew enough about firearms to make a decent choice, and since I couldn't tell a Glock from a Luger, speculation was pointless.

"As long he doesn't get arrested, I couldn't care less." I replied. Toddler rolled his eyes.

"He'll be fine man. We've done this before. Besides, everything he's doing is completely legal." Toddler acted as if Gabe had run to the store to get some milk, not go in to spend dirty money on a handgun. I was less comfortable. Nervousness surrounding drug deals was, for the most part, a thing of the past, but I wasn't a gun runner and still felt antsy when we made this kind of move. I played along because I wanted to get high, not because I had any real faith that what we were doing was safe.

I looked out of the car window at the flow of customers moving to and from the parking lot. Most wore holsters or slings and carried one or more firearms. There was more camouflage and full lips of chewing tobacco than I cared to count. These twenty-first century cowboys walked chest out, staring each other down through polarized Oakley lenses.

Toddler had come up with the idea of flipping guns shortly after Gabe started shooting up. Normally, when somebody turned twenty-one, purchasing alcohol was the main concern. Toddler's mind worked differently. He used Gabe's age to do things like rent seedy hotel rooms and buy the occasional handgun.

Convicted felons weren't legally allowed to purchase firearms, and most of the dope dealers we bought from had at least one felony charge. Aside from minor misdemeanors, our records were collectively clean, so we provided an essential service to the corner boys. Toddler claimed that as long as we didn't know for a fact that our buyer was a convicted felon, the sale was legal.

"How long do you think he'll be?" I asked.

"Who knows. You just worry about you and let Gabe do his thing, alright?" Somehow, Toddler always seemed to arrange these schemes with little to no work set aside for himself. I had bankrolled today, and was using my car to get us around. Gabe was using his ID to get the gun. Toddler was, for the most part, a bystander. I wished my mind worked the way his did so I could run the show. I wasn't a fan of playing the pawn. In spite of this, he kept me consistently high, so I didn't have much room to complain. So long as you did what Toddler suggested, you would end up high more often than you would on your own. It was a law as sure as gravity.

The car was beginning to get hot and the anxiety that came with the onset of dope sickness made the minute's tick by slowly. After a half hour or so, sitting in the car was more uncomfortable than going out to mingle with the flannel-clad inbreeds. Though Toddler and I were as far from fitting in as possible, we decided to take a walk around. After we had made it halfway to the entrance, I noticed the line at the door in front of a booth selling tickets.

My cash was with Gabe. I was close to turning back to the car when Toddler pointed at a yellow plastic sign hanging on a door off to the right of the main entrance. The black lettering read "Flea Market," and there didn't seem to be anybody checking tickets there.

"Let's see if we can get in that way," Toddler suggested, probably because he was as broke as I was. We changed course and headed for the smaller entrance.

Once inside, the whoosh of giant metal fans hanging below white fluorescent lights replaced the summer sky. The dull murmur of salesmen at booths and potential customers haggling over prices filled the air. The entire area was a maze of tables loaded with pocket knives, blackjacks, pepper spray, and other nonlethal weapons. It was hard to believe that there were people out there who made their living schlepping this stuff from town to town.

I realized I had lost Toddler somewhere in the shifting sea of gun nuts. I looked around and spotted him drooling over a packed table of spring-assisted switchblades and small electronic Tasers. Behind the table stood an overweight, red-faced man who could have used a shave. The salesman stood at his post, beading with sweat in spite of the industrial ceiling fans overhead.

He demonstrated a button-operated switchblade to a boy roughly our age. Speaking enthusiastically, he sprayed flecks of spittle over his range of products. His faded denim overalls fought to contain his gut. The boy who was the target of his manic sales pitch moved from the table, apathetic to the sputtering man. Without reacting, the man turned to survey the crowd and choose another customer to focus on.

His eyes settled on Toddler, who was looking at the Tasers with interest. For a boy of his persuasions, Toddler wasn't what you would call intimidating. Frequently finding himself in vulnerable situations holding drugs or money was enough to cultivate his desire to stay armed.

The salesman launched into a pitch, his rural drawl suiting his appearance. "You get zapped with one of these puppies in the gut and you're liable to shit your britches," he bragged, as if this specific trait was what one looked for in a Taser. The beer-bellied man behind booth picked up one of the black, plastic boxes from the table. It had two evil-looking, steel spikes the protruding from one end. Suddenly, a loud crackling erupted from the box and a jagged stream of white light came to life in between the metal prongs. Toddler turned and looked at me.

"Dude..." he said, grinning. The man behind the booth beamed, sure he was making a sale.

"You want to give her a try?" He said and held the box out towards Toddler, who nodded enthusiastically and reached out towards the man. The cracking noise came once again and the man made a short lunge forward. For a man of his size, he moved surprisingly quickly, connecting with the tips of Toddler's fingers. Toddler let loose an embarrassingly high-pitched yelp and jerked his arm back.

"What the fuck is wrong with you?!" he shouted. The man responded with a gravelly belly laugh. Toddler reddened and his voice went up an octave. "You piece of shit!" When his blood was up, Toddler lost his trademark social tact and in a room full of weapons, this wasn't the place for him to get out of control. I placed a firm hand on his shoulder to remind him of why we were here.

"You were the one who wanted to give it a shot," the man said, still smiling. Several of the customers moving from table to table had stopped and turned our way. All the eyes on us unsettled me. Attention was exactly what we were trying to avoid. I gave Toddler's shoulder a squeeze. I wasn't going to let him get any closer to the man with the knives in front of him.

I felt my phone buzz in my pocket. One hand still resting firmly on a tense shoulder, I checked the screen and answered with the other hand.

"Where the fuck are you guys?" said Gabe.

"We're next door at the flea market. You good man?" I asked.

"I'm standing in a parking lot with a handgun" Gabe replied flatly. "Get the fuck out here."

"We'll be out in a second. Just relax—everybody in that lot is packing. They don't even notice you."

Toddler had picked up on my side of the conversation and seemed to recall where he was. The fat man was already showing off a butterfly knife to a new customer. I motioned for Toddler to follow me towards the door. Walking quickly, we made it back to the Civic. Gabe waited for us by the car with a gun in a woven nylon holster in his hand. When we were back in the car, Toddler held a hand through the gap between the front seats.

"Let me see the piece," he said.

"Don't call it a piece. It makes it sound like we're about to go do a drive by or something," Gabe said.

"What am I supposed to call it?" Toddler asked.

"I don't know, man. It's a pistol, it's a gun. Just don't call it a piece."

"I hate to break it to you, Gabe, but that thing became a piece the second you paid for it," I said, starting the car and pulling out towards the main road.

Once we drove onto the highway headed towards the city, Gabe relaxed a little and passed the gun to Toddler in the back seat. He immediately took it out of the holster and held it up to the window sideways.

"What the fuck do you think you're doing!?" Gabe yelled back at Toddler, who giggled and made "brrrrat" sounds with his lips, aiming at a white Chrysler a couple lanes away.

"Keep that shit down man," I ordered. Toddler still laughed, but he lowered the gun.

"Dumb ass," Gabe added.

"Chill. It's not even loaded," Toddler said defensively, as if a cop would let us off with a warning because we didn't have rounds in the clip. For the millionth time, I wondered if Toddler actually was a legal adult or an 8-year-old masquerading as one of us, as his size suggested. I could see the gun in the rearview mirror. It was small and black, but I couldn't determine anything else.

Toddler was fiddling with the clip release in the back seat. Even if it wasn't loaded, the way he toyed with it sketched me out. I knew he could find a way to cause a problem even without ammunition.

"Don't shoot anything in my car, okay?" I said.

"Don't worry, man. The only thing we're going to shoot today is heroin." He held the gun to his inner arm, made a blasting sound, and slumped back in his seat.

I drove the car toward my least-favorite spot to cop in: Mosby Court. Downtown Richmond was beautiful as long as you stuck to the areas in and around the Virginia Commonwealth University campus. Stray too far away from the hipsters and art students and you had to keep your head on a swivel.

The dealers themselves were easy to locate but hard to maintain. They all used burner phones and changed them month to month. If you didn't build a solid financial report, you wouldn't have much of a chance to get the new numbers, and that meant starting over with a new dealer.

We exited the highway and skimmed the edge of the VCU campus. Black and gold banners bearing the head of the mascot hung from lampposts every few dozen feet to mark off the areas that were safe from those that weren't. The well-maintained roads and sidewalks were a testament to the millions of dollars pumped into the area by students convinced that their degrees would assure them a top-tier job in the adult world.

I hardly saw the students. My junky blinders were on. When it was time to get high, my eyes could only see dealers and cops. Gabe and Toddler shared my head space and the car passed quietly by as if the campus didn't exist. Toddler's normally jovial attitude shifted to a steely focus when we copped. He goofed around when we didn't have a job to do, but business was business.

Mosby Court was at the edge of the city across a bridge over the James River. As urban neighborhoods closer to the city center were gentrified, areas like Mosby seemed to go further downhill. The entrance to the area where we usually found dealers was in between the city jail and a little restaurant called Sandra's Soul Food. I took a sharp left turn and drove up the hill toward our destination.

All of our eyes were peeled for police. The street looked clear, but even if it wasn't, it would only have slowed us down for an hour or so. When it was time to get high, a one-track mind came with the territory, and at this point we were too invested to turn back.

At the top of the hill I slowed the car down. This was usually where we saw dealers waiting. Just as expected, two corner boys sat on lawn chairs under a tree not far off to our right. The ability to spot a dealer came over time. It's not something that was easy to explain, but when you saw one, you just knew. Toddler's senses were keen, and he had motioned for me to slow down as soon as I clocked the dealers.

Slowing the car to a crawl as we passed was all the invitation required for the man on the left to walk towards us.

It didn't matter how often I came down here, it was never exactly comfortable. Worrying about the police played a role, but that was a concern in anything we did, so I was used to that part of the fear. I think my real issue was rooted in the fact that I was vulnerable down here. In the West End, we didn't have to worry about much. If any of us got burnt, we could take care of it. Down here that wasn't even a consideration. It didn't matter whether you brought one carload of guys or three, we were hopelessly outmatched. As big as they talked, none of my buddies had the balls to stand up to dealers who actually used guns and didn't just sell them every once in awhile. No, if we were going to get fucked, there wasn't shit we could do about it and today, and it was my wallet on the line.

Toddler had the window rolled down. It went without saying that he would be doing the talking. Even with his pathetic size and young looks, he had a way about him that set dealers at ease. He arranged deals as casually as normal people talked about the weather. In a matter of minutes, he had worked out a deal to trade the gun for dope straight up instead of making a deal for cash and having to cop separately.

We pulled around and parked in front of an old house with boarded-up windows. I thought maybe this was the stash house, but if that were the case, it wouldn't have taken so long for our new dealer to come back. We waited for close to fifteen minutes. Just before I suggested we take a look around for somebody else, Gabe spotted the corner boy approaching from down the road.

The rest of the deal was standard procedure. I drove towards him until he could hop in the backseat next to Toddler. I continued to drive with the dealer giving me occasional instructions to turn left or right. As tempted as I was to look back at the exchange, I had to trust that Toddler had things under control.

"Yo, pull over here," came the instruction from the back seat. I obliged. We weren't close to where we had picked the dealer up, but this was safer for both of us. Seeing somebody get scooped up and dropped off by a number of different cars all day would alert any police watching the area. After some heated discussion, we decided to have Gabe cut out about a gram for himself and Toddler, leaving me the rest.

When my portion was finally in my hand, I wondered if it was worth all the trouble. Gabe and Toddler were a gram richer than they were when they set out for the day, but I could have easily just taken my cash to the corner myself and ended up with nearly as much. There was a point in my life when I would rather have a point and a friend to get high with than three points to myself, but that time had passed.

"How's it look?" I asked. Toddler and Gabe were digging into their heroin like children on Christmas. I usually drove, which meant I had to watch them get high before I had the chance to do so myself. I had taken bumps of coke and hits off a nitrous cracker behind the wheel, but I couldn't stand anybody else sticking me, so I had to wait until the car was parked to get my shot in. Gabe tapped his finger into his dope and touched it to his tongue. He nodded.

"It's decent," he said. I reached my own finger toward his bag.

"You mind?" I asked. He held his stash open. I tasted the bit of powder. When you got loose powder from different dealers and didn't maintain a consistent source, your taste buds were your best tool. Even without experience, it's easy to identify the flavor of baking soda or milk sugar and figure out what kind of cut you're dealing with. After some time, you can get an idea of how strong a batch is before you put it in your body.

I was of the opinion that if junkies took the time to taste their shit before they cooked up, they wouldn't be ending up in emergency rooms getting Narcan'd all the time. I took a great deal of pride in my pallet. If there were such a thing as a heroin sommelier, I'd be a shoo-in for the job.

Toddler cut about a quarter gram and scooped it delicately into the cap of his rig.

"Next time, we've gotta get two pieces. I'm sick of this small-time bullshit."

"How about you bring some of the money next time and we'll get three," I said.

I felt the chill of dope sickness creeping under my skin. When my bones sensed the presence of heroin, they creaked and whined for a hit of their own. The longer I put this off, the worse the stiff aches would be.

Toddler withdrew the rig from a trusty spot on the back of his hand, a bead of blood marking where the needle had been. I watched him as his head lolled back as if his neck could no longer bear the weight. His jaw slackened and dropped open entirely. My heart skipped with a violent pang of jealousy. I gave the Civic a bit more gas and rolled into the fast lane of I-95. I wasn't about to be the only sober motherfucker in the car.

CASUAL LIVING
LESLIE BOHEM

In the early 1970s a small condominium boom began along the Southern California beaches. You can still see some of these early signs of the blight to come as you drive along the coast. Most have been eclipsed by the much larger developments that have turned nearly the entire southern stretch, from Huntington Beach to San Diego and even down into Baja California, into one long, dull city. Some have been torn down, some have had their views blocked, and a few remain untouched; and now, through the strange lens of time passed, seem almost quaint and charming.

But in 1974, there were only a few of these complexes. They were new and, to a certain group of upwardly-mobile young people emerging from the haze of the 1960s, they were extremely fashionable. For a relatively small amount of money, you could buy a tiny piece of the California dream, as long as you didn't mind sharing it with a bunch of expectant singles hoping to find one last big party before they moved on to the things that would be more permanent in their lives.

I remember driving past these condominiums in those days, as they were being built, and I remember that they filled me with a vague nausea for the future. Through the empty sockets of unfinished windows, I would see the couple that in six weeks would be making love inside, watched by walls that hadn't yet been built. I would see the room, lit by the cold glow of the television left burning like a candle to light the sleeping lovers. I remember that the huge, concrete foundations looked more like a ruin to me than like the beginning of something.

I didn't trust the condominiums. Even then, there was a dreadful sameness to them and there was something more sinister. There was desperation here, as there is in most places that are dedicated to pleasure. A pathetic struggle against time. Off the tennis courts into the Jacuzzis, a generation whose single striking attribute had been Youth was clinging to its myth of difference as if a modern haircut and a connoisseur's knowledge of marijuana were proof that the revolution had been fought and won. It seemed to me that it was somehow worse to buy your jeans pre-faded than to have your Brooks Brothers suit tailored to fit. It was strange to me what my generation had become.

I think of all of that, still, when I drive past one of these now older complexes. But when I think about the condominiums, mostly I think about Page Alexander.

Page Alexander had been famous. He was a founding member of the band The People's Auxiliary, one of the score of semi-psychedelic groups that had flooded the radio in the mid-1960s in the wake of Sgt. Pepper. Page was the lead singer and songwriter in the group, and his very long, very unkempt bush of hair and huge wardrobe of lavender bellbottoms and paisley shirts made him its visual focus as well.

The band did well in California with their first single, "Timeslide," but what brought them to national attention was a cover story on the "Youth Movement" in *TIME* Magazine. The story featured a photograph of Page complete with Indian headband and love beads. For all his hippie accoutrements, he was a handsome young man. And that, of course, was what the media wanted.

In the article, Page was quoted as saying, "We spent twenty years in your world and we don't want it. Dylan and the Beatles have blown your cover. Acid and grass have turned us around. Rock and roll is our salvation. Some fat straight in a stay-press suit thinks he can tell us how to live. The joke is on him. We are living, and we're never going to stop, we are never going to grow up, we're never going to die."

The group's next single, "Your Mind's Eye," stayed in the top ten for three months. Several parents' groups applied pressure and a few stations banned the record, citing Page's obvious endorsement of dangerous drugs.

But by 1968 there were other bands, and a Beatles double album to buy, and The People's Auxiliary's second album didn't sell. Then the bass player was drafted. The group made a final appearance in a Russ Meyer movie and tried to find another bass player. Their recording contract wasn't renewed. The guitar player did an audition for a rock and roll TV series that was to be a more realistic version of "The Monkees." He got the part but the series was shelved before the pilot episode had been filmed.

Page Alexander recorded several solo albums, none of which were successful. He did one album with two other members of the Auxiliary and two members of Quicksilver Messenger Service. The album was never released.

In the summer of 1974, I was in San Diego visiting a friend of mine named Peter. Peter's brother lived in one of the new condominiums. It was in Solana Beach, just north of the University. He was out of town and Peter was house-sitting. The place had been built on a cliff above a private beach. It was all-natural wood and had been elaborately landscaped. All the units had been sold before the foundations were laid.

Peter's girlfriend, Sue, was also staying the night, and after dinner, the three of us went out to the Jacuzzi. It was a Saturday night and there were at least a dozen people in the little pool. Bottles of Perrier and José Cuervo littered the tile sides. We said a few uncomfortable hellos and wedged our way into the water. It was not quite hot enough.

"They turn down the temperature on the weekends," an overweight man with a sweaty red face said. Sue was very pretty and he looked right at her, staring even after he'd finished speaking. He had a gold coke spoon around his neck on a chain.

On the far side of the Jacuzzi, sitting on a deck chair by the swimming pool, a man was watching us suspiciously. He had a short permanent of tight brown curls, a neat little moustache, and dark aviator glasses. Even in the electric torchlight that glowed dimly from the walkway behind him, I could see that he was very tan. He was smoking a joint. I turned away from him. There were several conversations going on at once in the Jacuzzi.

A girl at the far end of the Jacuzzi was talking to her friends about a party they could go to in Del Mar. The overweight man with the coke spoon necklace was speaking to another darkly tanned man in his late forties with incredibly white teeth, which he flashed as often as he could. The overweight man had lit a cigarette and it dangled from his wet lips. He spoke in a loud, self-conscious voice, obviously meant to impress Sue.

"They're heavily into real estate, heavily. They own half of Venice and they're building thirty-eight units in Agoura. Damn." He had dripped ash into the Jacuzzi. He scooped it out with a little laugh and looked back at his friend.

"They got in on a good thing. Venice was strictly blacks and canal water; you could pick up a duplex for nothing. Now it's a big money game."

The man with the permanent drew on his joint and coughed. Then he came over to us.

"Excuse me," he said to Peter, "I'll have to see your key."

"What?"

"Your condo key. You guys don't live here, do you?"

The conversations all stopped. Everyone in the Jacuzzi looked at us.

Peter reached up to his towel and showed his brother's key. "I'm Gordon's brother," he explained.

"Gordon didn't mention anything to me about having guests."

"I'm house-sitting for him while he's out of town. Do you work here or something?"

"I'm the manager. My job is to make sure everyone follows the rules. Guests have to be cleared if the resident isn't with them."

"Are you the only person he would have told?" Peter asked, annoyed. "I mean; I have his key. I can go get my I. D. if you want."

The guy hesitated a moment, looking from Peter to the rest of us, his eyes pausing for a moment on Sue. "Let me check with the office," he said and he walked off towards one of the buildings.

We all sat for a few moments then in an awkward silence. The overweight man with the coke spoon wouldn't catch any of our eyes, in case, I suppose, we really were interlopers.

"Anyway," the girl at the other end of the Jacuzzi said, "they're going to have a live band in the disco tonight, if we just want to stay here."

Then the guy with the perm came back. "Your brother did speak to Lainey in our office," he said. He sounded a bit humiliated. "I'm sorry to hassle you, but we've had a lot of problems with crashers lately." He looked apologetically at Sue and, after a moment, offered us the joint. No one took it.

"Where are you guys from?" The Permanent asked, still looking at Sue.

"I go to State," she said.

He remembered to look at me.

"L. A.," I answered.

"Oh, yeah? I used to live up there." He waited for us to ask him about it.

"Really?" I said. Something about him had begun to disturb me, a vague familiarity.

"Yeah, I used to be in the music business. The trips got to be too heavy, so I came down here to mellow out."

"Page Alexander," I said then.

He was delighted. He even lifted up the aviator glasses. He looked at Sue, but she was younger, and had no idea who Page Alexander was.

MALT LIQUOR
GEORGE LOSEY

Fernando couldn't control his internal lizards, and this often led to trouble. He kept a zippered gym bag stuffed with moisturizer and stress balls close by at all times. When he was 9 he learned to converse with newts, geckos, and whatever small lizards he could get his hands near. By his eleventh birthday he'd been kicked out of his village for associating with such unconventional friends. His parents were decent people but couldn't find just cause to go against the villagers' wishes and soon, though disheartened by the loss of their child, they came to relish the peace and quiet left behind in Fernando's wake. No more late night bullfrog Strip Poker Parties, no more Russian Roulette with brontosaurs, and paramount, no grieving brontosaur relatives holding loud, interminable vigils for their foolhardy recently deceased.

They rented his old room to a troupe of traveling actor vampires who had sought out immortality to enable them to perfect their craft, though all that extra time only led them to become uncannily self-indulgent. Upon less than poor reviews of their, in all honesty, overwrought and bleak adaptation of

The Lion King, they wrathfully converted the town into their own half-turned unliving minions before being driven out by a team of hired mercenaries. Despite their gruff exteriors, the mercs hid hearts of gold, and once the vampiric menace had been dealt with, they stayed on to rehabilitate the spiritually lobotomized and train them as seeing-eye-persons. With the profits from their wildly successful business endeavors, they set up a first-class orphanage. It did Fernando little good, as he'd been gone four months by the time the tie-dye doors of Summer Of Love Orphanage opened.

Fernando went to live among the brontosaurs. They were kindly accommodating and each gave him one thing apiece so that soon he had acquired enough to live on for a week or so until he had things straightened out. They all smoked constantly and with difficulty. Half a dozen intrepid Bronts eked a living out of selling Bronto-Friendly cigarette holders. Competition in this market was fierce, and after a few years of pedaling only half-functional holders, the tech evolved at such a rapid rate that each brontosaur smoker, or every brontosaur, was easily able to put away a minimum of three cartons a day. As a result, the Bronto Village was enveloped by a solid fog of smoke.

Fernando, as a youth, and proportionally smaller Bronto, wasn't able to tolerate the cloud, although the bulk of it hovered more than a yard above his head. He eventually settled on the form of an Anole, and was able to avoid the smoke and sustain himself on the scraps and ends of the Dinosaur Bread he'd been given for a full 6 months. Conversation was difficult until he'd mastered the trick of switching between his Dilophosaur form (Dilos being known for their abrasive noisiness) to speak, and his Pteradon form to carry his Dilo self onto the necks of his Bronto friends. The Brontos were annoyed by the presence on the sensitive bits of their already constantly aching necks and began to resent him. Then, as per custom, they never confronted him directly, and instead shoehorned passive-aggressive statements between or at the end of sentences. Fernando was so distracted by his constant transformations that he never caught these remarks, or half of what was said to him.

Fernando's time in the Bronto Village came to an abrupt halt one night at a village meeting. The elders had heard disturbing rumors from the East regarding the spread of vampirism, his old town was declared the epicenter, and as a debate raged on the best way to contain the disease, he slipped out as a Chameleon.

He had many pointless and tiring adventures along the way.

Soon after leaving home he came across a nest of unprotected chicks. The three hatchlings' parents had been slain defending their nest from unreasonable tariffs, and immediately upon seeing their pitiable condition, Fernando resolved to intercede in their favor. In the forest nearby lived a blind tiger, Banjo, who was known to lend her aid to lesser creatures in exchange for visual assistance. Fernando came to her first as a tree frog. He echoed his greeting in an astounding manner capable only to those of the species, hoping to convince Banjo that the local amphibians had come to resolute consensus as to her role in the chick's rearing. Banjo, with her advanced sense of hearing and smell, was not fooled; she knew he was only one frog, and lackadaisically stretched her forelimbs, showcasing her impossibly sharp claws. "Why should I bother? These chicks are none of my concern. Let them return to the earth," and with that she made to leave.

Fernando, however, had one last ace up his sleeve; the nest was nestled at the top of a mountain range upon which grew a singular plant with energizing properties. Once he'd taken on his true form and explained the many ways in which the plant could improve her life and legacy, Banjo agreed to take in the little winged fools.

Banjo the tiger fought fang and claw to ensure the success of her ward chick's business. She slashed prices, passing the savings on to JavaChicks's horde of customers. When competition pressed in from the East, she mauled production costs and the company branched out to include in its leafy, bean-sodden tendrils a record label that only pressed music that was only tolerable while riding the brown bean, and otherwise sounded too inaccessible, and thereby intellectually avant-garde, trapping success on two frontiers.

The chicks soon won a T. V. deal, though at the time the oldest by 100 seconds, Jose Ruffolsio, was obsessed by the never im- or explicitly stated mystical truths of the yearly winter freeze. The glare of the sun on the frozen water formerly snaking past his home captivated him to such an extent that he refused to participate unless ice was made a focal point of the program. His younger brother was covered from beak to talon in obscenities that grinning foreigners had assured him were words of good luck and beseechments of cosmic favor, and was thereby not camera-friendly. The youngest, a lady chick, easy enough to look at, and spiritually non-dynamic enough to leave no bitter taste in Omnivision's board member's mouths, lacked the needed in-your-face brassiness that moved units. The program was eventually retooled into what the Omniboard hoped would come off as a surprising mix of Survivor: Fire Island and Mad Max. Feelings were discussed beyond their breaking point, and then meta-recontextualized until everyone everywhere was so tired of the whole thing that from then on out T. V. S, tablets, and all other screens only sprayed viewers with a burst of white to black pixilated explosion, and still the subscription fees flooded mail routes.

The youngest chick, crushed by the rejection of the viewing public, walled herself into a nest mound through which she regularly clucked orders to keep JC, running even after her carefree siblings had moved on to new whims. She contrived to grow more entrenched in the affairs of business, and thus a depressingly large swath of the outside world, even after flesh and feathers grew pale and then luminescent within her darkened sarcophagus.

JC had early on caught the attention of the newly renamed Summer Of Love Peninsula. Half the now go-getting, 20-to-early-30-something population really went in for the brand's lip-service take on environmental awareness, while the rest were so disgusted by the blatant addiction pedaling that they worked overtime hours to afford the extra Restull Tabs they constantly popped to keep from having nervous breakdowns.

To the East of the nest, a town flourished on with bent back and preternaturally rushing endorphins; SwaySpine.

Five years prior, while helping a newlywed mouse couple enjoy their honeymoon without the ever-looming threat of disembowelment, Banjo the tiger swallowed the owl mayor of SwaySpine. Osfred was stringy from long years of struggle overseeing the cultivation of the hard granite fields of SS, and flavorless from fretting over national debt.

When SwaySpine lost their leader, the land subcame to the charms of a scoundrel from the South who retooled the local elite into materialistic hedonists with a penchant for social subterfuge. All chairs made in SwaySpine were crooked at just the right angle to cause permanent and painful spinal damage. Demand fell, and with it price, so that by the next quarter, SS chairs flowed across the world, undercutting all other furniture manufacturers, and undermining the spines of just plain folks on all corners of the globe.

The carefully constructed granite mines were burned down to their opioid mineral elements, and under the rouge ken of Dolphyn Restfull Tab, production began.

The racket was a good one as long as it lasted. Just in time to cause mass addiction, the mine's minerals were sucked dry, and withdrawing TabHeads hopped up on JavaChicks brew descended upon SwaySpine, burning the town's renowned crafts district, and forming an ideology unfortunately initially engineered by Dolphyn himself who was one of the few not taken alive.

After leaving the chicks under the care of Banjo the tiger, Fernando traveled to the Archipelago Empire. On his second day lounging by the shore in the form of a garden snake, nibbling the edges of popcorn leavings, he was summoned to the royal volcano.

The Patriarch had heard tell of his transformations and hoped to confuse and stall the efforts of a witch seeking the servitude of his sole offspring, Too. The witch, having fulfilled her end of the bargain ages ago, waited patiently while the Patriarch paraded Fernando.

"Flash all the distractions you can muster the girl is, by rights, mine. No manner of spectacle will hold off the inevitable." The Patriarch smiled daggers at the witch, and while waiting for a stupendous feat from his guest, had his hopes of derailment laid to waste. Nanders made his introductions properly, but became transfixed by a closed cabinet. He opened it to peek inside and, recalling his good manners hastily, shut it with a loud snap. Quickly he reopened the drawer and delicately shut it again with an inoffensive click.

The patriarch, assuming his guest to be developmentally delayed, relinquished his daughter to the witch, and Too spent the rest of her days ecstatically changing colors into food.

After the islands, he sailed back to the mainland and lived on the plains. He came across a village and hired himself out as a dance instructor. After a few lessons, his hastily erected dance fort was filled with locals dying to be the first to decipher Fernando's ever changing dance. To keep himself in high demand, he would add new moves each lesson, and tweak the old ones just so that anytime a pupil got close to mastering the Living Dance, even their partial version would be outdated and incorrect. The dancer would be scoffed out of parties, and the daily noon dance-offs until they folded and returned to the class.

For once, Fernando was confronted by overwhelming success, and, bored, finally moved on leaving a disappointed little town in his wake. They consoled themselves with Restfull Tabs, and eventually JavaChicks beverages, which only furthered their voracious whimsies. Dolophynism hit the plains in a big way after his departure.

Next, Fernando met a wizard swaddled in garments that showed the night's sky. The old man's eyes reflected a star imploding in real time and when he said, "Come with me to my lair and you will see great things." Fernando didn't hesitate for a moment. On the second afternoon he spent following the wizard, they both caught an intestinal illness from a blue uncookable fish they'd drug out of the river, and had the stubborn temerity to eat even after unsuccessful attempts to fry, boil, and burn the thing warm. The only cure was four steady hours of firefly ingestion, and in the middle of that interminable ritual, while the wizard alternated from stuffing his mouth with glowing bugs and voiding his contents, Fernando finally asked what they were journeying so far to behold, and the wizard responded with difficulty, sweat trickling from his forehead, "a penis."

The wizard's stronghold was so vast and splendid that they spotted the tips of its towers and peaks while they were still a week's walk away. The ever-close, and yet not-close-enough spectacle was too much to bear, and by the time they'd arrived, Fer barely noticed the majesty of the stronghold and hurried inside to finally see the elusive penis.

Once through the many winding halls and staircases that led to the wizard's inner sanctum, the bristly-browed old man removed his spectacular robes, and our hero briefly beheld his penis. "But this is absurd!" Fernando exclaimed, "we needn't have come all this way for you to show me your penis. You could have shown me your penis on the plains, and we would have been done with it then and never needed suffer through this whole ordeal." He left in a fury of dissatisfaction with a vow never to go out of his way for no real reason actually ever again.

It was then he decided to visit his hometown once more before journeying into the interior and eventually far coast of The Continent.

Unbeknownst to him, the mother of his secret child died of frustrated longing the exact moment he resolved to return. June Swift had fallen hopelessly in love with Fernando from the moment she first saw him reaching for nothing in the air, moments after they'd been born simultaneously in the same cramped hospital room.

Initially, June tried to distract herself by doing the daily crosswords, but her appetite for his love was so voracious that even after her parents had exhausted their life's savings paying for newspaper subscriptions from across the world, and she had gone blind spending days and weeks on end orchestrating her own life-sized puzzles spanning the edges of first her, then her neighbors' property. June still burned with a never ceasing longing.

At the age of 16, blind as a crone and with a heart twice as careworn, she finally realized she'd never be able to distract herself, and with an entirely emotionally honest, if not perfunctory goodbye, she left her ancestral home and became a dish maid for the section of town where Fernando lived. Her nonexistent vision made it impossible for her to carry out her self-assigned task, except when it came to Nando's quarter-full and forgotten cups of water, which she could smell and feel from miles away. Under the guise of cleaning the dishes at her "headquarters" she'd steal away into the barely functional hovel she'd cobbled together for herself a short distance into the desert just outside of town.

She collected the water, which had briefly nuzzled his lips, and used it to nourish a solitary rose whose color she'd never know. Once the flower had reached maturity, she waited for a coinciding full moon and equinox, and saying the name of her love, tucked the bloom into herself. 9 weeks later, Little Swift was born.

June's mysterious child carried on her work and was so competent at it, having inherited the late miss Swift's stubborn tenacity and Fernando's bizarre luck, that SOL-Pens finally realized their need for a dish-cleaning service. Under June's watch, the town had become more overcome with soiled dishware than ever it had been stuffed with Bronto bones, which had all by then been both tastefully and tactlessly repurposed. The child's strangely colored eyes and personal lineage with the dish business kept off competition. Though he was only a small, and by all appearances well-mannered urchin, all but the foolhardiest dreaded to lock eyes with Little Swift. Housespouses became paranoid, women and men felt as dirty as the plates they'd send off to be cleaned, not only by an orphan, but one with magic sight that could read dreams and count bank balances with only a glance, and an entire side industry dedicated to pre-cleaning dish rinsing bloomed overnight. No one knew how Little Swift managed to clean so many dishes in so short a time; they never bothered looking into it, so distracted were they with Fernando's return and the mounting rumors of war.

Since the spring, Dolophyst sympathizers had been threatening to annex the mountains where the JavaChicks corporation lived. SOL-Pen hearts bleed for the people of SwaySpine, so ill-used by history, while at the same time they found the aggressive vibes too harsh to deal with. When every town had sided one way or another in the coming war except SOL-Pen, a representative came to demand their decision. He left 2 hours later, head still spinning with hundreds of flowers expertly twined about his boots, pants, bayonet, everywhere, even somehow his severely close-cropped hair. Both parties took one look at the hapless messenger, chuckled at the folly of peace, and opened fire.

Fernando immensely enjoyed the Twinning Ceremony, though he had no idea of the reason for it. As bombs detonated North, West, East, and South, of him, he decided he would work part time, just for a little while, just as a lark, cleaning dishes in the form of an elephant.

EXTERMINATING ANGEL
MARK BLICKLEY

They're hard to see. But you can smell 'em. Yeah, they're here alright. This is their most favorite room in the entire hotel.

Smell that? It's like rotting raspberries wrapped in a stanky sheet. You can smell it, right? It's the odor of indecency. Thought I got 'em all last week. Or most. And no one comes better than me, Crispin Colvin, exterminator extraordinaire! Damn straight! Know what my motto is? "My extermination clears a path to your liberation." Your liberation from fear, suffering, and infection,

I know what you're thinking. You're thinking: why does that fool spray all that deadly chemical and not wear a mask? A mask? I don't need no friggin' mask. I ain't got nothing to hide or be ashamed of. Purity protects me. Purity of essence!

You doubt me? You think I've sniffed too many fumes and delude myself that spirit is superior to body? My body of work speaks for itself. And I'm here to protect all of you from the evil that goes by many names chintzes, mahogany flats, red coats, wall louse, crimson ramblers. Yes, I'm talkin' bed bugs. Those little demons are masters of deception. Anywhere you can slide a credit card a bed bug could fit. They can flatten themselves down to fit in any crack or crevice. Feeling itchy my friends?

I'm like a freakin' suicide bomber willing to die for a cause or a reason in any season in order to flush away all of their bloodsucking trauma and filth. Filth, you say? Don't all the magazines and newspapers stories make a point of telling us that bed bugs aren't attracted to dirty, unclean, grimy places? It's true. They don't even inject any dangerous diseases in the warm succulent flesh they feast on. Your flesh. That's not their brand of torment. The filth I'm talking about is PERVERSION! A filthy perversion of body and soul! Your body and soul!

Do I hear snickering? Go ahead, laugh. Laugh and show your ignorance. There's a national epidemic of bed bugs in these United States of America, and not because of physical filth. It's because of moral filth. Within the fabric of American life are the crevices where these gluttons skulk and hide, waiting for the opportunity to siphon your blood to fuel the most despicable acts of sexual depravity this side of a Tiger's wood!

You ever hear the label scientists put on bed bug mating rituals? They call it

TRAUMATIC COPULATION! That's right. And do you know why they call it traumatic? It's because the male ignores the female's genitalia. Rejects her pathway to creation. He refuses to gently place his sperm into a female opening. Oh no. If they did that it would mean the males would have to court the females and show them respect by trying to please or appease them. The pen may be mightier than the sword, but not in the wicked world of bed buggery!

A male bed bug's sex organ is a weapon greater than my own. It's a long, sharp spear with a hypodermic hook attached at the end. The male pounces on the female, holds her firmly while she struggles, and then rapes her by stabbing his razor sharp hook over and over into her back, her stomach, any exposed area on her body. He stabs and squirts these huge doses of sperm directly into her mutilated flesh. If she's lucky enough that this mating wound doesn't develop a serious infection and kill her, then his seed swims to her ovaries. Every time he gores her flesh it leaves a scar.

I ask you, can a society that treats its females like this be less deserving of extinction? I am a warrior for righteousness.

Brace yourself, my friends. There are even more shocking perversions male bed bugs commit against all that is decent and true in nature. They indulge in bestiality. You heard right. Bestiality. Twenty percent of their sexual encounters are with foreign animals. The little hopheads will bang anything that even looks like a bed bug. These perverts have sex up to 200 times a day and they don't give a damn who it's with. These gangsta bugs spend their whole lives just stabbing and shooting, stabbing and shooting. They stab anything that moves with their pointed pricks and shoot a disgusting amount of splooge into whomever or whatever they gashand slash. If a male bed bug were human in size, he'd be shooting seven gallons of man milk with each ejaculation! It ain't human and it ain't decent. Killing them is a sacred privilege.

Domination! Abomination! Proliferation! Irritation! Aggravation! Defecation! Fornication! And Homo-gen-iz-ation of an entire generation of male miscreants!

Yes! Yes! Yes! These bloodsucking fiends engage in homosexuality more than any other depraved sexual activity. Fifty percent of their illicit intercourses are the rape of other males who have just sucked—your—blood. And when the sperm of the rapist enters the male, the jism searches for ovaries. When none are found it mixes with the raped male's man gravy and is passed on in his next encounter with a female. Sick. Sick. Sick.

You wanna scratch? You feel them chewing on your tender skin? Where's the itch? The itch is in their lust for your blood. They cannot indulge their dirtbag dicks without feeding on your juicy red plasma. They must feed on and steal your lifeblood energy in order to satisfy their corrupt desires. It's the warmth of your bodies and the sweetness of your breath that draws them to your vibrant flesh.

I smell them!

I listen to them!

I fill my weapon with venom and wait... wait... wait... wait...

PALETTES AND WHEELS
EMILY AUMAN

A faded, racist poster watched me from its red metal frame
on a wall the color of baby's first poop. I look down at
my hands because I don't know what to look at and I realize the nail polish I put on just two days ago, dark purple, is
already chipped and imperfect. It really doesn't take long for
that to happen.

"So I walk in this record store," The sight of his dark,
messy hair mixed with the context immediately reminds me
of John Cusack's character in *High Fidelity*, who somehow
manages to express every possible romantic hamartia in a
two-hour film, "and I'm flippin' through, you know, whatever." Eloquence is not Eddie's greatest quality. "The guy
who works there, he had this crazy beard and really thick
glasses and the guy looks at me and says, 'Wanna see something really rad?'"

I nod and widen my eyes to show interest.

"And he pulls this record out." He flashes the sleeve in
front of me, mustard yellow. "It's songs from 1970's pornos,
like, legit. Apparently some dude's dad used to produce the

music and he realized it would be a niche market to repro-
duce. There's only like 200 or something."

"That's really neat!" I do find it genuinely "neat," but
"neat" is also the word I use when I can't find the enthusiasm to match the other person. He nods eagerly and puts the
record on; slow notes penetrate the airways and I can sense
the vintage nudity in its tone. Eddie's lanky limbs sit down
on the couch a cushion away from me, the couch a faded
robin's-egg blue, and I sit with my legs curled up to my chest,
a cup of hot chocolate from my favorite coffee shop steaming
in my hand.

"So what do you want to do?" Eddie asks, glancing over
at me with long eyelashes and a crooked smile. I like Eddie.
He's the biggest contradiction I've ever seen. He's a challenge
to understand and I like trying. Handsome, intelligent, fun,
educated, from a respectable family: he's a waiter at a sea-
food restaurant (who ironically is barely keeping its head
above water), he drives a scooter, and his favorite movie is
Starship Troopers. He is the only person I've ever met who
continues to surprise me.

"Oh, I don't know. I'm up for anything." I too am a contradiction. I am both a free spirit and guided by strong moral
principles. I am both independent and the neediest person
you will ever meet. I am what many label the "Manic Pixie
Dream Girl."

"Wanna go to bed?" The best thing about Eddie is when
he says something like this, he is not using this as a thinly
veiled attempt to get me to take my clothes off; he really
means *go to bed*.

We curl up in varying snuggle positions on his cream
colored sheets and tell stories. I love to tell stories. He also
obviously loves to tell stories. He has a lot more stories than
I do because not only is he a few years older, but he has also

lived, hence the scooter. Within a week of our acquaintance, I had heard about his brief days as a synthetic acid dealer. I do mean literal days. "I made hundreds on hundreds in that week, let me tell you, but once a stranger calls your number, knows your full name, and asks for drugs, you know it's best to stop while you're ahead."

His eyes change color a lot. Usually they are some variant of green, but today they're gray.

We fall asleep. We always fall asleep, just curled up in each other's arms, fully clothed. I twitch when I'm first asleep and it scares him every time. "It's really aggressive! Like you've just been stung by a giant bee!" He told me this once and I giggled because of his ability to sound like an adult and a child at the same time. All of his stories are told this way, like when he explained the time he spent a week in jail for drinking and driving. Eddie, while describing his incarceration, actually said, "But the guys in there? They made me a dream catcher out of a cup and threads from their clothes. Isn't that so nice? I still have it." He does. It hangs from the ceiling in his bedroom. It is black, white, orange, and very tattered looking.

His apartment is muted and shadowy because it's surrounded by trees and there aren't many windows. In the middle of the day, you have to use a light to get around efficiently. So we usually lie in the dark and we sleep. When we don't sleep we tell stories. When we don't sleep and we don't tell stories, I ask questions.

"Why do you like me?" Needy. Our vision is very well-adjusted to the dimness on this sunny Tuesday afternoon, so I can see his expression. He runs his lanky fingers up and down my spine through my tank top. It's hunter green.

"You're nice. I don't think I've ever heard you say anything mean about anyone. You're so pretty, like, you clearly have no idea how pretty you are. I don't know, maybe you do. I mean, I don't know how much we really have in common but I think we both really appreciate the earth. You don't think dolphins have superpowers or anything do you?"

I laugh, "No."

"You're smart, too." He stops here. Good enough, I guess. He hugs me close to his torso and kisses my forehead. My cheek is pressed against his baby blue dress shirt, a button pushing into my upper lip. "Are you going to stay the night?"

"No." Independent. He runs his fingers over my porcelain shoulders.

"Okay. Do you like me?" He asks, I see his face fall a little.

"Obviously." I get up and slide on a sweater, the brown of an autumn leaf, and my boots of the same color. I see my nail polish got chipped even more today. I need to just take it off.

"Why?" He turns over in bed and watches me, one hand under his head. I can see what he looked like as a little boy, conspicuously inconsistent, large eyes rimmed with black lashes, the little gap between his two front teeth more prominent, his skin extra dark from summer break.

"Because you're colorful."

EQUIPMENT
DAVID CROUSE

Each object resided in its hidden place in the house and also in his head, as if he owned two of each thing: the one in the bottom drawer for use on evenings and weekends and the one at the back of his mind he could take out on a lazy Thursday afternoon at the office. The second had gained weight with the ticking of years, but the others were still there, and could be lifted and held when tugged from beneath a mound of balled socks. The paddle board with u-rings at either end, the pink sticky tape in its heavy pack of three, the pony harness hanging at the back of the closet wall, the butt plug with the plume of silver tail, and the purple ballet boots thrown in a pile with her five pairs of striped running sneakers. The heavy human yoke and the first hood she no longer wore because she said the insides smelled like a hockey mask, a whole hockey team, and she laughed as if the joke had surprised her. The feathered whip and the rubber bindings and the choice between black ball gag or yellow, large or small, like choosing between coffee or tea after dinner, paper or plastic at the grocery store, cereal or oatmeal, as they entered another morning after almost two decades of marriage.

He was trying to find a particular thing, but his own brain organized itself against him. The day had been long and his tooth ached from the lemon seed stuck at the back of his mouth since that agonizing business lunch. Everybody with something witty to say about food and politics and that week's episode of whatever, but it was all the same thing, and none of them knew about her and even if they did, what would it change? He pushed the shirts out of the way, hangers scraping along the metal rod, to the panic snaps in their plastic bag and the knotted wax sheathed rope in its cardboard box marked *happiness* in red marker.

The Chinese needle nipples, the clamps purchased from various hardware stores for a buck or two and rung up at the register by an unsuspecting clerk, the three-hundred-dollar cat suit with the zipper up the back where it always should be, because a zipper on the front spoiled the smooth effect and made you look like an amateur. But where was it? There it was. He gripped it in his hand, and everything became simple again. The future stood as simple as an unlocked door. Again and again with the feathered whip across the naked buttocks until she turned over and stared him down from behind the mask studded with metallic nubs, lips bright red because otherwise the picture was not complete and he couldn't get off no matter what and she couldn't either, because her following him had become a habit.

His hand would rise up and he'd speak one of the words for her, something soft at first because waiting was good. Then down again with a flash of the wrist, almost without effort, as if turning the page of a badly written book—again, again, again, and then enough. There was an art to inflicting the damage, a line between good pain and bad. He had always prided himself on possessing this particular skill, like a person who knows some delicate trick: fly fishing, preparing crepes, speaking a dead language, but the last time, more than a month ago, his hand had felt like something apart from him, a thing he had to lift along with the whip, and tonight he was more tired, more dispirited, than even then. He slashed a line down and across the empty air. He could hear her on the stairs and then the bathroom door.

The hesitation before fastening the clamp to her right nipple. The slivered twist, like tightening a tap to prevent the wasteful drip, drip, drip. All of this would happen soon, and before or after that the pause and drink from the glass of apple juice, the t-shaped spinal bar making her motions vaguely robotic and ludicrous. He wore a mask too, crowned with chrome thorns he had fastened to it himself almost a decade ago when he had been more ambitious in his sexual life, less ambitious in his work at DuPont Chemical, where for the last five years he had luxuriated in a corner office and a heavy wooden desk with Pepto Bismol and anal beads in the bottom drawer.

She could tie her hair up and take a shower in a few minutes. That's what she was doing now. He could hear the hiss of the hot water, the sliding of the curtain. He held his mask in one hand, the leather mitten in the other. He was making a mess while she tried to bring herself back to order. Home from Brigham and Women's again and that was always what she did, the water across her face and chest just long enough to soften her skin. He thought of calling out to her, but why? And what would he say? That he cared for her and loved her and that everything would be okay? She'd look at him as if he'd just gone insane, and anyway, it was important for her to have that special private time with her own body, especially now.

The water stopped and he stood waiting for her in the future. The recitation of familiar nasty words as he brought the lash along her reddening skin, each word drained of meaning after years of use, but still capable of surprising him once out of every fifty when they came to his lips (and hers too). Some of the best words, like *dummy*, had a humor to them, but darkness somehow greater than an overused swear word. He liked to say, *hey dummy, do this*, or *hey dummy, do that*, her eyes always bright and intelligent behind the mask unless she willed them to dullness. Sometimes she seemed to be listening intently, waiting for that one time when the insult meant something and her actor's gasp became a real one.

The way her shoulder blades tightened with each fall of the whip, and the big black dildo waving cartoonishly in her fake frightened face. She needed this and so did he. He had reprimanded someone that morning, gently, but she had curled her lip and pleaded with him not to file the paperwork. He had felt as if he had struck her across the cheek, this single mother with shoulder pads and poor organizational skills. The daughter he never had? She had vacation photographs hanging in her cubicle, from *Ohio* of all places. He gave her another chance, feeling like her persecutor and savior all at once, and then he checked his messages to see if she had called, which she had, and the message was not good news. No specifics on his voicemail, but he could tell instantly.

So he needed the weight of the handle in his hand and the vibration shock moving into his body when it came down, and he needed the ball gag opening her face to him and the crown of spikes. When he had been thirteen, he had found a bent roofing nail in the small square of his parents' suburban yard, and had put it in his pocket and felt the beginning of his strength and his separateness. It had pinched his thigh as he moved through the school halls, and years later the idea of it became this thing he wore openly in his bedroom with her. In all of this lay the possibility of a new idea, a slight variation that would tickle some animal part of his brain, wake them up, and push them past love into a more precise and effective feeling.

The tomography scans and intracavitary brachytherapy, the bright blue catheters, balloons of salt water, and radioactive pellets sometimes called seeds and sometimes called bullets—what business did science have creating such stupid metaphors? They had run her small and naked through a long white tube and sent signals through the center of her. He remembered the beep and then the deep groan of the machine. The noise reminded him of a noise made by something else in a factory he had once worked in as a teenager, a thing designed to crush garbage. He made another slashing motion through the air. Finally, he called out to her, "Are you ready yet?"

He heard the toilet flush. He dropped the mitten and held up his own black mask and looked into its skull. Soon he would be in there.

She yelled back, "No soap. What did you do with the soap?"

"I bought liquid soap," he said. "It was on sale."

He pushed the tendril of waxy rope through the u-rings and the other ends to the harness, but then he remembered the leg bindings curled in the basement on his tool bench. His mind felt like a fumbling, comedic thing, a clown moving in slow motion, when it was supposed to be a knife. She appeared naked in the hall except for a white towel draped around her shoulders and chest in the way a matador might wear a cape. Her legs were wet from the shower, slick, and probably warm to the touch. She could open them and he would cherry-stuff the marbles, a different word with each one, except her face had the expression of oh, wait. Somehow they had surprised each other. It was as if she had caught an intruder in her house and she was calculating the odds of escape. He couldn't find a way to slot this particular scenario into the complex array of fantasies that occupied the back part of his brain. When he was fifteen he had tied his own hands to see how it felt. His mother bought him a book on magic, the great Houdini and his many escapes, and was glad to see him take an interest.

"I couldn't find the other mitten," he said, and he sounded like that child from long ago.

Her nakedness made him naked. It was as simple as that. He was instantly aware of his flaccidness inside his boxer shorts and chinos, his paunch lifting his tie slightly. For years it had fallen straight as a noose, but not these past two or three. He smiled to see her. He wanted to apologize for everything, but one of their rules was never to do that. That was something for other people.

She said, "It doesn't matter."

He had kicked off his shoes and tugged off his socks but somehow forgotten his tie. The mask puppet capped his hand. He held it from the inside and his voice, the voice of danger, was still in there waiting for him, but he spoke in that other voice, the everyday voice of cubicles and overseas phone calls and light reprimands of incompetent employees. "You surprised me."

He knew she felt the same thing. The shock was there on her hard face. He had always admired her high cheekbones and Roman nose, but it all turned a just a bit ugly when she was upset, and she was on the verge of that right now. "Put in on," she said. "Please."

"I've had a bad day," he said.

"Take it out on me," she said.

A sliver of invisible will extended from her to him as a finger to a wound, probing and waiting, and then retracting when he shrank away from her.

At eighteen he had told his first girlfriend that sex was boring and he wasn't going to do it anymore. She told him he was probably gay. At nineteen he had found the roofing nail again, in a box of toy soldiers, and moved it to his jeans again. His parents had divorced by then and he was going through his old things. He thought of the nail the first time he bit her hard enough to bring out blood. She had said, "I want you to bury me." This on their first week knowing each other. It felt like those six words might be enough to build the entirety of their lives on, the way others build lives on religion or property or the futures of their children. The groan of the machine entered his mind again, as if from the other room.

"Take it out on you," he said.

She could spin and run and be gone before he took a step. The towel would fall from her shoulders and he'd bend and pick it up while she crossed the living room downstairs. It would happen: the wrist straps and delicate tongue bar, her voice making mewing sounds. It was the least he could do for her. The clamp was on her right nipple, but that would make him think of the missing left. She dropped the towel from her shoulders, but of course she didn't run. Her body, five feet long if you exaggerated, which she liked to do because falling short of that five-foot mark—and announcing it at a party when someone remarked on how small she was—made her feel like a child. Not a child, she said sometimes, a boy, someone wearing a baseball cap and talking about superheroes. Years before that it had been a point of pride, her boyish figure moving through a pool as she swam laps, but now it was the worst kind of insult, and after the surgery she began growing her hair long for the first time since she was a teenager.

When she returned home from the hospital after the surgery he had rubbed the right nipple and told it he would give it double the attention. Now they inserted plastic tubes and talked about realistic expectations.

The scar stretched across her left side like a torn envelope, a fist-sized bulge of flesh and muscle remaining around her armpit. A blank space where the second nipple should be. At seventeen he had sometimes thought about making love to an armless woman, squirming beneath him like a worm. At least he wasn't stupid enough to believe this was some sort of punishment for sinful thoughts. She had taught him that lesson, pulled him out of Catholic suburbia like a goldfish from an aquarium. Sometimes he still remarked with amazement, *she picked me.* Her body moved across the room as if on a wire. He did not like to put his mouth to these places. The scar had become a line of demarcation between her body and something else, a different body created by other men who told him, "She is very lucky."

They called it the shark bite to good friends and to each other, and sometimes she even told the false story of the teeth closing around her chest and dragging her under, the blood forming on the surface of the ocean. For some reason she was let go and she floated to the surface. "And then you dove in and found me," she would say with a sly smile. "I remember you grabbing my arm and I thought it was the shark again, but no, it was you, pulling me to shore. You saved me." He didn't know how to read that smile. Was the lie funny simply because it was a lie, or was it the nature of the lie, the great shark letting her go? The absurdity that he would be the one able to dive in and save her while danger still pushed through the water below them?

"The shoulder harness," she said. "The mask. The ankle T-bone."

"I was going to buy a new one," he said.

"A what?" she said.

"A mask," he said.

"It's fine," she said. "It really doesn't matter."

He was on the verge of apology. He tried to think of blackened matchsticks touching her shoulders. He found himself fumbling with his pants. Their bodies came together, but they came together hard, and she began to say the nasty words, *stupid* and *bimbo* except they sounded about as nasty as the words *refrigerator* or *television* or *sleep* or *retirement*. She said, "Take me to the bed. I want you to punish that part of me that hates you. There is a part of me that hates you and it needs to be snuffed out before it grows."

"I can do that," he says. "I know exactly where it is. Did you think you could hide it from me?"

They held each other under the covers, both naked now, and the hood sat at the bottom of the bed: a lap dog waiting to be called up to them. He could feel her body shiver with anger. It radiated outward at the blandness of the world, the house they rented between two other identical houses, his forty-seven-year-old body and his childish brain, which was thinking tedious thoughts about paperwork and the single mother he had given a second chance. Her face had been so grateful, an animal stretching for a kind hand. A line had been crossed. For the first time he had wanted to fuck someone else, not as a game, a thing they said to each other, but for real, right there in his office. He found himself caught up in the pure rays of his wife's anger and he wished suddenly that he had written this other woman up, raised his voice to her, told her that she *was on thin ice* or whatever moronic thing people said in those situations. *He would be keeping an eye on her.*

The chain was cut to be exactly the length of her body, so it could be draped across her from her foot to the tip of her skull, over her face, dividing her into two parts. The weight of it made her wet and the sight of it made him want to tug it off and make her whole again, then divide her with his cock instead. The hoods purchased for forty and forty-five dollars eight years ago while on a trip to New York, the sweet feathered whip, the melted oil pooled in the small of her back. Once he had placed a paper cup of grape juice there as she posed on all fours and told her not to move.

"Catherine," he said. "I'm falling asleep. I'm falling asleep on you."

He knew she was wide awake. He held her body and it was as stiff as metal, as a corpse. His hand found her ass and he began to grope, but the action was a mechanical reflex, a twitch, as he spoke from the new Swedish mattress. His words seemed like twitches too. *Tired. Bad day. I love you.*

That was one of nasty words. *Corpse.* Also *sex corpse* and *dead woman,* as in *I'm going to fuck you like a dead woman. I'm going to kill you and then you'll be a dead woman.* For a while—for years—it had seemed like these words had placed them into an exalted state, and all the rest of it—the newspaper on the front porch, the grass grown too long in the front yard, even the rooms they moved through with their imperfect bodies—was an illusion. He said, "We should book some tickets. I don't care where. Just book some tickets and let's go. Someplace warm. I don't care." He found himself saying that again. "I don't care. I don't care." A child's expression. The thing you scream at your parents. He said, "Do you remember the thing I told you about the roofing nail?"

"Yes," she said. He felt as if he was sharing the nail itself, the original object, found somehow right there on the bedroom floor. "I was jealous of that nail for a long time," she said. "I wanted to live in your pocket and pinch you every time you took a step. And nobody would see me."

"I'm falling asleep," he said.

She said something, but it was whispered too low for him to make it out. She said it again more loudly and this time it registered. "You need to tell me what to do. Why don't you tell me what to do anymore?"

"I do," he said. "I left that voicemail for you today. I told you to masturbate. I was very specific." But he hadn't. He had thought about it briefly as he knelt to the water bubbler, Jason Fitzgerald still talking while he took a long draught. Then they had resumed their walk down the hall and the thought had been put aside.

Her body peeled away and scrambled to the foot of the bed and he decided she might be heading off somewhere to touch herself. But she returned to him, the hood in her hands. "It's been so long," she said. "Please." She pushed the hood to his face. It touched him, a second face against his mouth. Ah, he thought, this is how it must feel. The mask pushed against him and he turned his head to the wall. "You'll feel better," she said.

"Why not just kiss me?" he asked. He felt as if he was speaking to the window.

"No," she said. "Never in this room. We promised. It's even more important now. We have to send a message."

A message. Where? To whom?

As if she had read his mind she said, "To all of them. They know about us. They don't know what exactly but it bothers them. We've found a loophole and they hate us for it."

He had never heard her talk this way before. Always it had been just the two of them, a private arrangement, a common law marriage, no children, no life insurance, no mortgage, and no kissing except on rare occasions in public, no *I love you* or *honey, how was your day?* But when he rode the elliptical bicycle at the gym lately he sometimes thought *love, love, love,* as if he were counting out the revolutions of the pedals. He thought of the shark beneath the water and counted and when he was done, twenty, twenty-five minutes later, he hit the showers and found his own body beneath his clothes, a flabby thing but unmarked except for a childhood accident to his knee resulting in a thin white line becoming visible as the rest of his skin reddened in the steaming water.

The riding crop and tongue clamp and the waist cinch. That little intake of breath as the red ties tightened. He took the hood again and felt the weight of its history, the habits of almost two decades. Then he turned the open hole of a mouth away from him, opened it, and lifted it above his head. He tugged it down and felt the authority it gave him. He also felt a little sick. He had grown lazy, selfish, and undeserving, but when he spoke next his voice had the timber of the old days. Before the shark attack, he thought, and he smiled from behind the leather. "There you go," she said, "and now say the words."

He said the nasty words and he felt himself grow larger in stature. They faced each other on the bed, their bodies lit by the hallway light. She looked around, found her hood, and lifted it up. It came down over her short graying hair, her suffering face. Behind there somewhere was the woman who had cried that it wasn't fair. Now she was just a pair of eyes and a mouth. Where was the lipstick? They needed the lipstick. They assessed each other as they always did: as enemies. She rose up in challenge and he read deeper into the script. She said, "If you kill that secret part, the rest of me will belong to you."

He remembered his watch. He had failed to remove it, and his hand moved to his wrist to correct the mistake. He let it drop over the side of the bed. He pushed the pillows aside too. The lump of flesh and muscle. The feathered whip and the dildo in its black case, secreted there like family jewelry. He held it all in his mind just as the house held it. All of it was available with just a toggle of one thought to another. She looked at him through the holes of the mask as she applied the lipstick in a messy 'o' shape. He liked it messy and so did she. She made her eyes big and stupid as she ran it around and around and around. She was going to die and then he would be alone and he was fat and lazy and did not deserve her. He said more of the words. Each one built on the one before, the rungs of a ladder that lead down, step by even step, to a place where they used to live, and where they could live again if he would just get his act together.

If they were lucky, he decided. Which they weren't. Maybe they had been, but not anymore. When he was nineteen he had looked into his heart and decided it was not the same kind of heart beating in the chests of others. When she was sixteen, she had watched Charlie's Angels reruns and imagined herself as one of the three, always the one at most risk. Her hair changed in style and color. The punishments would become increasingly violent. She would be one of them except she would lose. That's how the story would end. She had told him all of this across the table when they'd first met and he had laughed.

The idea was to live forever in that secluded place. The rest of it was nothing. You traveled out into it on various expeditions—on visits to family, to work, to the treatments—but you looked through it as if through a liar's words as he tried to convince you of something ludicrous. And it *was* ludicrous. Her missing flesh was ludicrous. His four-hundred-dollar watch was ludicrous. That he could own such a thing and she couldn't own a piece of herself. His voice spoke more of the nasty words but his cock wouldn't rise to attention. The spikes crowning his mask were a poor substitute. They had not worn their masks in a month and a half.

He put the wrist straps on her one at a time, jerked them tight the way she liked, and then he held it hard by the back of the neck. Also something she liked and he did too, but it was hard for him. He knew that it must be harder for her down there, beneath him, as he roughed her to the new bed. The submissive had to be strong because everything was built on that person's back. Their lives, their *real* life together, always rested there. It still did. He brought her down but not roughly enough. It had been better years ago, when they were poor and he was still getting his MBA, and she was getting her MFA, and they did this on the floor of a one-room apartment. But that wasn't true; he was sentimentalizing the past, which was something they had agreed never to do. He put on the clamp and gave it a slight twist. "How does that feel?" he asked.

"More please, sir," she said.

"Three pleases," he said, so she said it three times and then he yanked it. She cried out and he suddenly felt like he was the one who should have escaped down the hall. Her lips curled a little to one side, and he thought of stroke victims and their bent faces. Instead of saying I'm sorry he twisted it even harder and said, "Say it like you mean it."

She said it again.

He saw himself from the outside in, a body wearing a mask, huddled over another body, and he said, "Not good enough. You are in danger. Don't you understand? I could hurt you if you don't please me. You're helpless."

She said yes and yes and yes. She knew that.

He sobbed behind the mask. She couldn't see what was happening except that maybe she could. Her eyes followed him. He raised his voice to almost a holler. So what about their neighbors? Their teenagers yelled louder when mom and dad weren't home. Their dogs barked louder and their riding lawnmowers buzzed louder on the weekend mornings when the sun intruded into the bedroom. Tomorrow they would go to Brigham and Women's again and the doctors would cut her again. Then they would see. That was the best they could do. He hollered, "You are a piece of meat. Do you think you can stand up to me? Is that what you think you can do? Because you can't. I'm going to squash you like a bug."

Yes, yes, yes.

"I am your king," he said. "Your life is in my hands. I can rub you out the way I would rub out a cigarette with my heel."

The sentences were wrong, tone too elevated and voice off, as if he were reading from a book instead of speaking from that cavernous place he had discovered through her. But he would keep trying. That's all he could do, right? "I can rub you out like a cigarette. Flick and grind. That's what needs to be done with a person like you. A piece of trash like you. Rub you out." He thought of something else, decided not to speak it, then spoke it anyway. "Do you understand me? Your blood stops pumping when I say it stops pumping. Understand me? Do you understand me? If I want it stops now or it goes on and on. Do you understand?" A look in her eyes of genuine fear, but there were as many kinds of fear as there were kinds of jelly beans: fear of being misunderstood and fear of being understood, fear of pain and fear of embarrassment. She had told him she had suffered through a happy childhood, ridiculous early romances. She had not believed there might be another like her out there in the flat world.

She said please ten times. He said not loud enough. The mechanical teeth spreader with the archaic winding motion purchased but never used. The yellow ball gag. The whip and the chain. He said not loud enough and he said she needed to be put in her place. He was crying hard and he nuzzled his face to the envelope scar. It was exactly like that: the thing you do to open the letter's seal and take the words out. The place where the shark had penetrated flesh with its serrated jaw. Except it had only released her so that it could arc out through the water, turn around and come back, its dead black eye taking her in. He pushed his tongue out through the mask and probed the flat surface, the raised line. He searched up to the armpit and he was hollering something, some kind of command, but she was kicking her legs. He yelled, "Do you think you could escape me? There's no way to escape me." Because that was what she was trying to do: run away into that other world they had long ago agreed did not include them, the land of weddings, funerals, insurance claims, polite co-workers saying I'm so sorry. "You will never get away," he yelled. Her feet kicked beneath him in a mad swimming motion. The voice came from that place they had built together, where the black equipment was always neatly arranged and new. "Never get away."

And then something he hadn't heard in years. The safe word.

In the early days they had chosen many words. This one was simple. It was like naming a pet or a child—the first rule was to do no harm—and so they had decided on the word "stop," which is what she said. Except that he didn't. It took him a split second, a darting motion of the tongue, before it registered fully. Then he obeyed. He lifted his face up and closed his eyes. He was surfacing hard. He took a deep breath.

At least she didn't have to repeat herself. He made a low snorting sound from behind his mask as he pulled thick fluid back up through his nasal cavity. This was a way of restoring his features to order, his brain too. The array of objects both large and small sorted themselves back into a neat arrangement in some lonely compartment in his mind, rows of them stretching into shadow. The rules of engagement were simple and clear. He rose from the bed. In the morning they'd head again to the hospital for the thing they had once been told would probably not be necessary, so early that she would bring a pillow and sleep in the car, slumped against the window. Who were these other riders on the highway, moving with their headlights on? Nothing to do with them except that they probably thought they were special too for whatever reason: their children, their salaries, some unique way the world cradled them.

He fumbled with his mask. He wanted her to see his human face. But her hands covered the wound; they did not reach for her hood, and it seemed like something they had to do together or not at all, so he lowered his hands and they faced each other in costume, each breathing hard, assessing each other as athletes. She had been a runner, was still one, although of much shorter distances, a painter of abstracts, and a lover of animals. Once before they had met she had climbed Mount Washington alone and hiked the Appalachian Trail, and she had a revised thirty percent chance of survival, as if she were a part of some great army headed off to war. Most would not return.

She breathed hard and deep behind the mask, settling back into her arms and legs and fingers and toes. "Let's try again," she said. "Kill it."

The ball gag to put the mouth at rest, the hood to calm the mind, the straps to still the arms and legs, the clamps to induce shivers of delight and misery.

DEATH PITCH
MIKE SHERER

"I want to kill myself."

A young man sits at a desk with a phone headset perched upon his close-cropped hair. He is squeaky clean, so bland he fades into the pale walls of his small cubicle. "Can you tell me why?" he speaks calmly into the microphone.

A dull female voice answers."Nothing is right. My husband is always gone. The few times he stays home usually ends up with an argument and him hitting me. My children are strangers. One day last week my son walked into our apartment and I didn't recognize him. I have no friends. The women I know are like me, zombies, and the men I meet fuck me once or twice, then disappear. Every day is the same. I sit inside and stare at the TV or at the walls or out the window. And when I go out, there is no-thing better to see, only ugly things and cruel people."She pauses, not even a sigh."I can just see no reason to go on."

"Have you tried talking to God?"

"What God?"

"You mean which God. The religious diversity of our nation offers many paths."

"Religion offers nothing to me."

"Then reflect upon the secular aspects of your life. Think back on all the people you have encountered, all the places you have seen, all the experiences you have had. After doing this, can you honestly say there is no reason at all for you to continue living?"

"I've thought everything out already. I want to die. That's why I called you."

The young man sits up a little straighter. A gleam comes to his eyes, and his voice gives away his interest. "All right. I am required by law to make a reasonable attempt to dissuade you. I have done that. Now we may proceed. As I'm sure you know, the Right To Die Act gives each individual the right to take his or her own life. This is how it should be. Your body belongs to you and it should be your decision what to do with it. What else, besides the opposable thumb, separates us from the animals?"

The young man pauses. The first trimester of a smile forms on his thin lips, and the timbre of his voice moves a note up the scale."My firm helps people carry out their very human right to die. I will personally guide you through the next difficult days. I will handle all of the legal details, something I am certain you have no desire to do. You are aware, of course, that the government will award ten percent of the estimated sum they would have doled out to you had you lived to life expectancy to any person or organization you designate as your beneficiary. The government does this because suicide, in these stressful days of overpopulation, scarcity, and pollution, is considered a brave and unselfish act of patriotism. I will see that your beneficiary promptly receives every dollar he or she is entitled to. Do you understand everything so far?"

"Yes."

"Good. Now under the Right To Die Act you also have the right to choose the means of your demise. Public suicide is illegal. Jumping from a window or a bridge, onto subway tracks, or in front of cars endangers innocent people, and no awards will be granted by the government for such a suicide. The same for drowning, since people unaware you are attempting to end your life may endanger their own by trying to rescue you. Also, discharging firearms, misusing prescription drugs, inflicting traumatic situations upon innocent bystanders by hanging yourself or slashing parts of your body with the intent to bleed out are also illegal. Your right to suicide does not give you the right to inflict pain and suffering on those around you."

The young man tones down his delivery."Of course, the government provides painless lethal injection for a peacefully quiet suicide. But as you intimated earlier, your entire life has been peacefully quiet, so you may wish to end it with more of a flourish."

He pauses for a reply. Eliciting none, he continues, his voice resuming its previous lively lilt."I can help you with this. My firm has connections with movie studios that are in constant need of suicides. Since passage of the Right To Die Act, stunt men are no longer employed. Why fake it when you can have the real thing? Imagine yourself in a western. Picture yourself as a sturdy pioneer woman in a cabin with your husband and children. Savages attack. Your husband is killed. You hide your children, then, in order to lead the savages away from them, you run outside. They catch you. The camera zooms in for a close-up of your face as the tomahawk strikes. The savages run off with your scalp. Fantastic! Not only do you bring your empty life to a thrilling conclusion, but you are an actress in a motion picture. Haven't you ever dreamed of being a Hollywood actress? And you won't even be bothered by the reviews. You won't be around to read them. So not only do you experience an exquisite expiration, but your death is recorded to be viewed by millions for all of eternity. To be digital is to be forever. Of course, the movie studio pays a substantial fee to your beneficiary."

"I don't know."

"There are other options. There are theaters that pay an even larger fee and can provide an even greater thrill. In such a theater you would have a live audience witnessing your very dramatic final moments of life. I say very dramatic because such theaters provide firing squads, hangings, beheadings, crucifixions, burnings at the stake, quarterings, stonings. The selections are nearly as boundless as the human capacity to inflict imaginative deaths upon one another. Imagine yourself dressed in all the splendor of Marie Antoinette, surrounded by a very realistic set depicting Revolutionary Paris, kneeling at the foot of a guillotine, awaiting the whisper of the blade slicing through the air, the first touch of steel on the back of your neck. Breathtaking! So. What do you think so far?"

"I... I don't know."

"This may be the only real choice you have ever had in your life, so think it over. In the meantime, there is one other matter for you to consider. The disposal of your remains. Because of the high value of land and the poor quality of the air, most burials and cremations are no longer permitted. Only the very rich can afford to be buried and only those who die by disease are cremated. The bodies of all others are recycled. But if you choose to end your own life you can choose to what use your body will be put. I will handle this for you. You may donate your body to science for research. Imagine!

You might accomplish something worthwhile with your life after all. There is also a market for clothing and jewelry and other works of art fashioned from the bodies of suicides. Just think, something beautiful could come out of all your misery and suffering. So. What would you like to accomplish with your body?"

"I... I have to think..."

"Of course. Now as for my fee. My firm collects ten percent of all funds paid to your beneficiary. This is a pittance considering the services we render and the peace of mind you will possess at the time of your passing stemming from the certainty that your loved ones will be well cared for after your departure."

"Yes. I've been thinking. I think I'd like the theater. And I'd like to donate my body to science."

"Excellent choices."

"Only nothing too painful."

"A beheading, perhaps? I've heard you don't even feel the blade."

"Yes. Marie Antoinette. In Paris. That sounds nice."

"Of course. Now, if you could come into our office sometime to sign the legal forms I could get the ball rolling. Do you know where we are located?"

"Yes. How about this afternoon?"

"Great. Ask for Larry. And please, if you know anyone contemplating suicide, tell them about us. We are not allowed to advertise, so if we are to continue to provide the very necessary services we provide, our only means of communication with the public is through word of mouth. From satisfied customers. While they are still customers. Before they are satisfied. Completely satisfied. If you know what I mean."

"Yes."

"Good. I'll be here until five. I'll look forward to see-ing you." The connection is broken as the woman hangs up. Larry turns to his computer and brings up the many legal forms.

As he begins filling them out, another young man leans over the top of his adjoining cubicle." Did you net a lem?"

"She had one foot in the sea already."

"A woman? You lucky dog. Where's she headed?"

"The theaters."

"Did she sound sexy?"

"Doesn't matter. The theaters can make any woman look sexy."

"Where is she headed after that?"

"The labs."

Shaking his head in disbelief, the young man remarks, "The stage! I haven't gotten one beyond the needle in weeks. You get all the weirdoes."

"Now give credit where credit is due," Larry responds, stroking the front of his neck." My golden chords." Still shak-ing his head, the young man drops back down into his cubicle.

Larry fills out the first form and half of the second by the time he receives another call." I want to kill myself."

DUMMY
DOUGLAS MILLIKEN

All the way from his house in the hills down through the
river valley, Richard hacked and pointed his directions
while beside him I listened and got us where we wanted to
be. The streetlights were off but some passing cars had their
headlamps on. Just south of town where the river widens
and skinny young trees are all that remain after last year's
clear cut, we pulled off in a wide gravel turnaround and I
nosed the old Chrysler to the west. Through the bug-stained
windshield, we watched the sun melt to fade out behind the
shadowy knuckles of the mountains. Waxy purples and pinks
flared through thin clouds, wispy as fading ghosts. Richard
lit another Parliament 100 and nodded while the light slowly
seeped out of the world. Like he was in negotiation with
what we saw.

On the radio, David Allen Coe was hating again. When
the sun was all gone, I started the engine and Richard resumed instructing me as to where to go, what turns to take,
and which fire roads to follow up the mountains. I didn't
think the Chrysler should be taking on such rough terrain,

but this was Richard's car and he was calling the shots. We rumbled under redwoods with our headlights slashing wild shadows through the trees, then crested a bald summit. We had a clear view of some other little valley town and beyond that—thick reds and yellows burning over the world's most lonesome blue The sun set for us a second time.

I took five bucks out of my pocket and told Richard to go fuck himself. Then I gave him the five bucks. But anyway, the money was already his. I was holding for him. The dollar lay right where I left it on his leg.

Neither of us said much of anything after that. I guess Richard just now and then would kind of laugh. Deep and wet in his chest. We'd argued about this before but now we both knew. He was a wizard.

You once told me that there are stars that shed no light. You told me I was one of those stars. So I can't know whether you'd be surprised that I made it this far west. Winter came on hard in our northeastern city and suddenly living outside didn't seem like so much fun—down in the tent-city, among the burnt out wreckage of the old harbor front, the snow piled deep in a single night, crowding against the naked poplars and the wandering haggard men all bleary-eyed with Thunderbird and the shock of being, their shambled lamentations rising in blue plumes from fetid, black-stained mouths—and with nowhere else to go, I made up my mind to head south. A couple crust-punk kids I knew were going to hop cargo trains all the way down to New Mexico, and somehow they'd found it in their hearts to invite me along, but I knew too clearly that during that kind of journey, someone was going to get hurt. Lose their legs or simply just die. If I was to be of that party, I knew: I'd be the one who'd go under. I think they understood this, too. To them, I'd be the lucky rabbit foot that kept them safe. I'd be the one to feed the rails. I respectfully declined their offer and left them with the uneasy job of sorting out who'd be their charm instead. Then I scraped together what cash I could and bussed as far south as the lines would let me.

My plan might've been to make a solid go of it down in Florida, eating oranges and sleeping on white sands, but I only made it as far as Georgia before things got kind of hazy. There were guys running crystal across state lines, which unleashed a fluttery moth of fear somewhere inside my solar plexus, but then again, also afforded me an opportunity to get around and see some country. A New Year came and went while I played copilot in the South. Then one runner—a self-styled greaser kid in an unlikely blue Gremlin—decided he didn't need to make the drop; he'd just keep going, make a fortune for himself somewhere else, and without even trying I found myself a quarter-share deep in the Carolinas. My logic at the time told me that this was too far north, so I sold the bulk of my stash in a fire sale and hitched west. I was hoping for some baked-clean desert, but instead I hit Oregon in shell-shocked confusion with my veins stripped and scoured. My last ride was from a trucker who hadn't slept in years, it seemed, and who opted to dump me at some reservation casino alongside the highway. My luck could've been worse. I washed up in the bathroom and hung around the tables, thinking that if I looked like a gambler, I could maybe score some free drinks. But this was a dry casino. I frittered and grew antsy, and I remember the ceilings seemed too far away, and at some point Richard saw me. He was working over a blackjack table, frustrating the dealer and making a fortune, and after buying me breakfast and correcting my coffee with a flask from his jacket pocket—and, more to the point, after arguing over the likelihood of the Celtics making it to the playoffs and whether they'd ever definitively get one up on the Lakers—we struck a deal that cemented our friendship. I'd help him get around and manage his self-medications and anything else he might need. In return for these services, he'd put me up and keep me in whatever chemical haze best fit my predilections. I've been living in his basement ever since.

After our second sunset had passed, we drove back into our valley town and bought fried chicken in a bucket from a drive-up window then went back to Richard's. While I fixed us drinks—nothing special, just tall glasses of bourbon and water—Richard took off his leg and got into bed. Then he called some girls. I really wasn't interested in all that, so I put some chicken on a paper plate and left the rest with the old man. His pipe was already smoldering with Ready Rock and ash, acrid smoke spinning dizzily in the air. On the TV, a derailed train puked fire somewhere outside Reno. Richard puffed and wheezed. I took my dinner to my room downstairs.

Long before all this, Richard had been an engineer at a GE plant outside of Troy, New York. He did that for twenty-five years. He had a wife and family I guess, but when he retired, he left it all behind. Maybe the transition from a daily purpose into infinite leisure made him crazy, but I don't know. These are just things I've pieced together from living with him. Or maybe I'm just projecting. Richard doesn't talk about that life very much.

From what I've gathered, he traveled around for a couple years, then bought this place in Oregon about twenty miles inland from the coast and a thousand miles from anything else. He says he loves the perpetual spring here. Always cool and misty and green with new things that are alive. But sometime soon after moving here, he wounded his leg doing something in his garage. This part of the story always changes, which makes me wonder how much of it is truth—and anyway, it didn't heal right, so by the time he went to a doctor, it was too late. Now his right leg ends just below his knee. It was probably around that time that free-base became an interest for him. As for the girls, I imagine they've always been a hobby.

Down in my room, I ate my chicken and drank my bourbon and watched a program about dinosaurs on TV. Having television was still a novelty for me. I'd watch anything and be amazed. In those days, every aspect of normal life impressed me. Dishwashers and pay-per-view. The simple luxury of a bed. For too long, I'd been absent from these things. I was still giddy at being invited back in. After I watched a stegosaurus stomp around for a little while, then the doorbell rang and I went up to let the girls inside. They were pretty the way these kinds of girls always are, which is to say, in spite of themselves. Behind them, a black car was parked on the street. Seeing it there made me think of hard-shelled ticks or those fish that sucker to the bellies of sharks with their mouths like cup-shaped razorblades. I knew it'd stay there until the girls came out. I closed the door and pointed up the stairs, but these girls knew the way. They'd been here before. One of them I recognized, but the other girl could've been anyone. They tottered up the stairs on unsteady heels, calling Richard's name, and I ducked back into my room. I ate my chicken and finished my bourbon. It made me want another. I waited until I could hear them up there, then I sneaked into the kitchen and fixed another drink and drank that down quickly. I hardly noticed the taste before it was gone. My eyes felt fuzzy, but everything else rang sharp and cool. I was clarified. I trotted down the stairs and back outside.

Not that much time had passed, but already, between letting the girls in and stepping out now, it'd turned from dusk to full dark. And too: it was raining. The sound was like dust popping on an old record in the quiet parts between songs. Except for the lights in the houses around us, the night's darkness was a pure and living thing. It felt viscous. I knew the black car was still out there, but I couldn't see it. I wondered if the driver could see me. Blind and maybe unseen, I waved.

I guess Richard must have once had a son. Back in his other life, back in Troy. Richard never mentions him, but there are pictures on the wall. Department store portraits. A boy at eight. The same boy at maybe twelve. Blonde hair and nice sweaters. The sort of pictures that tell you exactly nothing about a person. A whole life of imaginable potential. It's very much possible that his boy would be my age. Which I guess, in its own way, might explain why I'm around.

For my part, I've never told Richard about you. The life I had, and how it was lost. As far as he knows, I've always been this way.

I said earlier that I live in Richard's basement, which points toward a certain image that I think is probably misleading. It is a finished ground floor with its back wall built into the hillside and most everything else above ground. There are windows. In the daytime, it's bright, and aside from one room Richard uses for storage, the whole downstairs is mine. I've a bedroom and my own bath and another room I don't know what to do with yet. I can use the kitchen upstairs all I want and anyway, Richard and I hang out a lot. There is a chair next to his bed where I sit and watch TV with him on the days when all he wants to do was lie around naked and smoke crack. Sometimes we hang out on the balcony and look out over the valley, drinking and talking or maybe saying nothing. In a way, the whole house is kind of mine. But it still feels weird living anywhere again.

Coming in from the rain, I wandered among my few things for a while until I found a tablet of motel stationary and started to write a letter to you. I wanted to tell you about seeing the two sunsets today. Instead, I started right in telling you about Dummy.

After spending the better part of the winter down South, I hitched around a bit and for a period of weeks found myself in Montana. It was springtime and kind of ghostly in those cool dim days of April, and the town I was in played along with this feeling. It'd once been a copper town but the mine went bust sometime back in the early 80s, so now all they have is a Superfund site. I guess most of the people there left when that happened. Now this pretty western town is almost empty. For me, in that season, it all just fit the mood.

I'd fallen in with another group of men like me, guys who maybe once lived somewhere and did work for money but couldn't do that anymore so did this instead. I'm sure we all had our reasons. At the edge of town was a half-built high school—something that was started during the copper boom but then left incomplete when the mines closed and everyone split—where me and the other guys slept most nights. It was clean and warm and empty in there with sheets of plastic flapping over the unfinished inside walls. It was a fun place to live. During the days, we'd just kind of wander around town.

I know these are things you don't want to hear. They don't really fit the details of what a "good" life is supposed to be. But these were okay times for me. For that little while, I was fine. And anyway, there's something I'm trying to say.

For whatever reason, that season in Montana, I found myself often in the company of this guy we only ever knew as Dummy. He was young and gangly and looked an awful lot like a skeleton who couldn't understand what you were saying. I'm sure Dummy was smarter than he looked, but that really isn't saying much. He'd grown up somewhere raw and poor in the mountains of Kentucky or West Virginia. He liked to swear but didn't really know how. He considered himself a lady's man, though as far as we could tell, he was still something like a virgin. To match this image of himself in his head, Dummy liked to maintain what he considered a clean look. Often we'd find him in one of the cavernous locker rooms—the cold water, for whatever reason, still ran—shaving his head with a played-out disposable razor. But he was bad at it. His head was crowded with scabs.

Dummy was a good guy, but he talked a lot, and some of the other guys hated him for that, but he and I got along okay. He didn't have to tell me his story for me to know he'd always had it bad. Someone else had made him this way. He could talk all day and it wouldn't bother me. It's not like I had anything better to say.

One time Dummy and I set out to find a ball because I wanted to teach him how to free throw and pass, but we didn't have any luck on that account. What we did find, though, was a kid's BMX bicycle abandoned down by the park. It looked like it'd spent the winter in a snow bank, its chain all rusty and tires a little flat, but it had

*pegs on the front and back. We could both ride at once.
I peddled first, and Dummy got on back. We rode as far
as the tennis courts, and then we just kind of stayed.
Dummy was laughing like I'd never seen or heard before. It was like when a dog discovers the moon and
then that's all there is in the world: just the moon. He
was hypnotized by the moon of his laughter. He couldn't
stop. I peddled us in circles and figure eights around the
courts and Dummy held onto my shoulders and laughed
and howled and shouted and laughed. I could hear him
echoing off everything. He was everywhere.*

I set down my pen and looked at the paper. I didn't want
to say what had happened to Dummy after that. What those
other motherfuckers did. He was a good kid and didn't deserve what he got, and I didn't want to think about finding
him that way. So I reread the last thing I wrote and remembered him laughing while we rode together around the nets
and between the painted lines. Then I told you that I loved
you, found an envelope, and licked the seal, and it was done.

Upstairs, it sounded like they were having lots of fun. I put
on my shoes and stepped back outside where the rain had
slowed a little, but the dark was still indelible and thick. It
took a long time to find the mailbox. I dropped in the letter,
raised the flag, headed back up the drive, but along the way,
I saw the dome light glowing inside the black car. A large African man was sitting behind the wheel. Light shone off the
smooth bald cap of his skull. He was reading.

Back inside, I headed for my room, but Richard must
have heard the door because he shouted my name and then
the girls started in too.

"Coleman," they yelled, then Richard said, "Coleman, get up here," and then the girls again: "Come join us, Coleman."

I normally didn't hang out when there were girls around, but tonight I was feeling funny, having thought about Dummy and thought about you, and I really wanted some company. It was nice of them to invite me up. In Richard's room, they were all in bed together and everyone still had their clothes on. They were just hanging out. It looked cozy. They were sharing a bottle of cheap red wine and passing around the pipe. They hadn't touched the bucket of chicken. On TV, kids were doing things with skateboards. They clearly weren't very good. The girl I didn't recognize smiled sweetly at me and told me to join them. She batted her lashes and everything. I stood for a moment near the door, then sat in the chair beside Richard's bed. They laughed.

The girl I recognized had been here a few times before and one time we'd got to talking. She used to drive a school bus up in Juneau, she'd said. Now she was here doing this. Just like the rest of us. Richard was sitting with a girl on either side and the girl I knew was the one nearest me, so she handed me the wine then handed me the pipe, then Richard offered his pack of long white cigarettes, and even though I don't smoke, I took one of those too. On the TV, a kid skidded off a railing and landed on his face. The girls were doing things now but Richard and I were playing it cool like nothing was going on. We were arguing as to whether Rajon Rondo would ever statistically beat Magic Johnson in consecutive double-digit assists to become the best player alive—but when the girl I recognized slithered between Richard's knees, I remember, like it was beyond his control, the bald stump of his amputated leg slowly rose from the sheets like a quivering hand raised in surrender. It was a little obscene but a little bit beautiful. In my lap, that sweet other girl was doing her thing to me. I was eating a leg of chicken.

"He'll never do it," I was saying. "He loses his cool too often. He'll get in a fight. They'll eject him from the game before the records ever broke."

They were swinging this baseball bat around and laughing when I came down into the gymnasium. There were maybe four of them. They were taking turns. I asked if they knew where Dummy was, but they just kept on laughing. The bat was filthy. I got on our bike and pedaled out into the drizzling grey morning, and it wasn't too far away, along the edge of the access highway, that I found him. His legs were in the road but the rest of him was in the ditch. It kind of looked like his head was hidden in the marshy grass. I knew nothing was hidden down there. They'd been thorough. I got off our bike, then I got back on. He was still holding half a candy bar. I peddled to a truck stop at the edge of town where the state road meets I-90. It was the same place I'd landed when I first found myself in this town. Everywhere I've gone and every stupid thing I've done since you sent me away, and only now as Montana gave itself up to rain did I feel like some vulnerable pink animal clinging to the face of a rock spinning through outer space. The only thing that'd changed was my knowing it. I walked around until I saw the pay phone, but when I had the black receiver in my hand, it hit me that there wasn't anybody for me to call. Dummy didn't have anyone in all the world. And the cops likely wouldn't get up to anything good with his body. Maybe it was better he stay there, I thought. Like a dog that'd been hit, or a raccoon. Some birds would find him. I thought maybe that'd be okay. I hung around the truck stop for a while, then I found someone who'd take me west. The truck stop had great coffee and was named Theriault's, and the driver didn't say one word to me all the way to Oregon, and it didn't hurt my feelings at all because I didn't want to talk anymore.

That's the part I didn't want to tell you. But now you know. I'm sorry.

Sometime much later, after we'd all passed out wherever we sat or lay, I woke up to a knocking at the door. Not the door-bell: a knock. It was the African man. He wanted me to let him in.

Standing there with each of us on different sides of the same open door, it occurred to me that he and I were en-gaged in the very same job. Each of us protecting the bodies with which we'd been entrusted. The same way Richard was protecting me. The same way everyone is protecting and pro-tected. All at once, we have power, and we are powerless. We only have to slip up once to fail. This man—twice my size and of a world so much harder than mine—could snap me in half if he wanted to. But this was my house. I told him he couldn't come in. I told him to wait here. Then I went up-stairs to get his girls.

It isn't just yet but it'll be pretty soon. Richard will get dressed up in his powder blue suit and attach his metal leg and go back to the dry casino. He'll clean house. He'll walk out with pockets full. Before he leaves for the casino, I'll ask if he needs a ride and he'll say no, "I'm feeling lucky tonight," he'll say with his voice a smoky mess, "I'm going it alone." He'll leave and I'll wait and the night will get late and at some point, I'll know. He'll be waiting somewhere, biding his time, and I'll know. I won't linger too long once I figure it out. I'll pack my one bag and I'll head out into the night.

But that night isn't here yet. I still have time. For a little while longer, I'm saved.

SLUDGE PEOPLE
GEORGE LOSEY

They walked the tended path to the shore as Donovan's foot began oozing out of his bleached white sneakers a few yards in the group of four distractedly dropping threads of conversations behind them in the short space all languidly flitted through like bread crumbs to either be rediscovered later and followed out or carried away by red brown animals and forgotten he had amassed an unsightly clump of dead leaves and twigs and bits of chitin from pieces of bugs no longer just background protein and structures reawaiting assembly whenever. They slowed Madison pretended not to notice after considerable readjustment an ample 30 or so seconds anyone still in their 20's for god's sake and with some remaining modicum of control over their own bodies would find more than suitable Donovan was only at best sloppily contained originally pale orange stained a rust gray and flecked with dirt and debris peeked through the seams in his shoes and Madison pretended not to notice with dread even

a little was starting to muffin top over the rim of his white
ankle socks.

Madison would have cared but she had been distracted by the
tickle in her throat coming from the disappointing unamusing
cheap pink plastic sunglasses she had in an accident driven
through her brow slowly making its neon trek through her
face that should be out again by morning given proper pos-
ture bumping it into her open medicine cabinet door which
had been left while trying with her anxiety skyrocketing all
the time and only adding to the crippling indecisiveness to recall exactly which order to take her prescriptions in because
some needed an empty stomach and some on a full one but
no trans fats rich fullness that she knew for sure. Also others could not be mixed within four hours of another or her
blood sugar would send despair dependent tendencies flood-
ing her with the sort of self defeating impulses and negative
situational cynicism that could have her skin dangerously
porous in just minutes but that nicely offset the unfortunate
bouts of excessive eagerness she sometimes experienced as
a result of another pharmapsychologically murky at best
contraindication.

The sun was already drooping under the horizon by the time
they had left Kenneth's vehicle the exasperation spread evenly
between them from aborted and continually reassessed and
retooled attempts at shared experience their eight hands
could not seem to work out how to grasp firmly all at once
anymore and silently some markedly more taciturn or falsely
jovial than others agreed to share the disappointment of

poorly laid plans and maybe grow from the adversity rather than further tax themselves or their already fragile group confidence. When they made it to the seaside, the night had begun, so they squinted and talked quieter knowing it would not help them see any better feeling obligated by the innocence of the whole thing to at least make effort to pretend Donovan was relieved by the dark especially relieved for him was Padty the youngest and furthest from dissolution and so squeamish around frailty but looking closely was ruled out when the peak of Donovan's chin had started to stream down in a stringy slim rope of dripping onto his collar bone he was happier than he had any right to be.

THE SUN IS CHIRPING / THE BIRDS ARE SHINING BRIGHT
ALAN WRIGHT, REBECCA HARRELSON, AND MATT ANKERSON

Tiny, sharp-edged slits of awareness peak through cotton balls and gauze. The sound of my alarm is somehow both muffled and piercing. I try to hit snooze, but it isn't there. Where the hell is it? Fuck. Why did I drink last night... why did I drink so much? What the hell happened?

When I say, "I rolled out of bed," it's not an expression, it's an adventure. Not too long ago I woke up next to someone whose self-esteem had to be lower than mine. It plummeted further once she noticed I'd baby-proofed the corners of my nightstand. Fool me once, motherfucker. I'll take embarrassing foam corners over stitches any day.

Today is a pretty successful dismount. I'm not gonna lie, I walk to the bathroom with a bit of a swagger. Actually, now that I'm more than a few steps in... It might be a limp. Yeah, definitely a limp. Whatever. I exited that bed like a boss.

It isn't until I've showered and brushed my teeth that I realize it's still dark outside. What the fuck? I don't stand for many things, but if I were to write a manifesto, I'd pretty much lead off with sleeping late. So why am I assessing my bruises at 6:00 A.M. and not the more civilized hours of P.M.?

The bruises are interesting, though. Highlighted by the extremely bright, yet environmentally sound fluorescents, the brownish yellow marks around my left bicep were clearly left by someone's strong, yet delicate hand. Strong because I see her fingerprint, delicate because I see the imprint from her lacquered nails.

My right ankle bitches at my full weight, which explains my early morning strut, and my left knee is banged up all to hell. Inspecting my puffiness, I vaguely recall a pretty intense tumble down a flight of stairs. I smile a little thinking about it, so I know that was something I came out on top of, even if I can't remember exactly who or what inspired that nifty little bit of choreography.

Was that an extension of the fight that led to my bruises or something altogether different? Why was I fighting a girl anyway?

On the positive side, I potentially had two different fights last night, but still have all my teeth and no bruises on my face, so I'm thinking it's a win.

Still no explanation for being up so early. Maybe I'll just get back in bed and call it a fucking day.

Just as I start to pat myself on the back for a day well given up on, the doorbell rings and I remember why I am awake.

Fuck ... for a brief moment I feel as though I am going to vomit, but swiftly remind myself I have no time for that. I throw all the clothes that smell faintly of sweat and alcohol into the hamper.

I pull on a fresh shirt from the floor. Whatever; it has to be cleaner than the one I passed out in.

The doorbell rings again and I take a deep breath. One of those breaths that therapists tell you will calm your whole body ... but they never fucking do.

I go downstairs, quickly light the candle on the table by the front door in hopes it will start removing any regret floating in the air. I breathe deeply again and open the door.

"Hey, Mom! Sorry about that. I must have overslept a bit."

I say this as I feel the acid in my stomach mixing with the bottle of gin I drank last night. God dammit, my ankle feels as if a part of the bone is missing. At this point I'm embarrassing myself.

"Come on in. How was the drive?" I ask her as she starts to analyze my entire being before even entering the house.

"Hi, Sweetheart ... " She pauses, then walks past me looking at the candle.

"Brian ... you look rough ... are you ok? I mean I have to ask, Honey. I'm not trying to be rude but ... you ... didn't relapse last night did you?"

Well shit fuck. She's been here less than five minutes and I'm already giving off the "I don't have my shit together" vibe. Probably because I obviously do not have my shit together.

"Jesus, Mom, of course not!"

At this point in my life, lying is like breathing.

"I was just up really late last night covering a show. Here—let me make you some tea. I'll run back upstairs and freshen up, then we can head to breakfast. Sound good?"

I'm definitely going to vomit when I go back upstairs. I make a mental note to run the shower to cover any dying animal sounds that I may exude.

"Your hair's wet... Like you've already showered..."

"It didn't take. Be thinking about where you want to eat." I move through the living room.

"Alright … Sounds good," she says with what I can only assume is doubt in her voice.

I nonchalantly look around the house for anything incriminating. Thank god I cleaned for this moment exactly before going out last night. I swear I am my own enabler. I put a pot of water on and the tea bag in the slot, set out a mug, and tell her to help herself when it gets hot enough.

I make my way upstairs, cursing in my mind. My body feels as if it's been hit by a truck. I change out of the basketball shorts I threw on in my panicked state, spot a new bruise, shake my head, then down four Tylenol and step into the bathroom. I turn on the shower for the second time this morning, and steam starts filling the air. As soon as I feel bits of water ricocheting off the tiles, like clockwork I proceed to vomit …

My shower resembles a scene only Lucio Fulci could think up. I stay put any way, resting my head up against the tiles, and slowly adjust the shower knob to a cooler temperature. I shut my eyes and begin thinking how great it would be if this day could come to an abrupt end.

My thoughts are interrupted by the sound of my phone ringing from my bedroom. Who do I know outside of my mother who would be up at this hour on a Saturday, and what on Earth would they want to discuss? I find myself longing for a few additional minutes of time alone naked with water pelting my head, neck, and spine. I decide to stay put in the shower.

My investment of additional shower time comes at a loss. My phone continues to ring. I converse with my mom from the shower and a floor apart, insisting and eventually pleading with her that she doesn't have to answer my phone.

I dry off, throw on jeans and a black Beatles T-shirt, and begin the search for my phone. I take a glance in the mirror to ensure I look somewhat presentable. I catch a glimpse of John Lennon in the reflection of the mirror, staring at me while trying like hell to hold in his laughter for what I assume are a number of reasons. At this point, it would be helpful to the search for my phone if the person would call back. They don't.

After a few minutes of wandering aimlessly around my room, I begin to feel somewhat anxious about Mom sitting in my kitchen, making for an easy out from my half-hearted search. Just before walking out of the room, I hear the faint ringtone my phone makes when receiving a text. It is coming from the vicinity of my bed.

There it is, lodged in a small gap between the mattress and headboard.

Before I even have the chance to swipe my finger to see who called, the phone rings again. The incoming call is from my friend Chad.

"What?!?" I answered.

"Is this how you answer your calls now?"

"It's not even 7:00 A.M.! Why the fuck are you calling?"

"Relax... And you really need to learn how to better handle your liquor. It's not like you had enough practice over the years, plus you hardly do any drugs anymore ... and by drugs I mean the types we ... well, you know."

"Chad listen, I have had a shitty morning and my mom is downstairs waiting on me to head to breakfast. Can we catch up later? By the way, why are you up? I don't remember much from last night, but I do remember you having your fair share of shots..."

"Brian, did you forget I have kids? The fuckin' four-year-old wakes up ready to go like he has a company to run, and the other two are also awake chatting with each other at a decibel only used when trying to have a conversation in a convertible speeding down the highway with the stereo blasting. Plus, I have to prepare for the line of questions about to be fired my way from the wife, who wants to know the details from last night. I will give her Belichick-like answers, frustrating her into giving up when she realizes any follow-up questions will be a waste of time. That's why I am up ... I am always up. I love my wife and kids, but this early morning shit they pull cuts years off my life. Anyway, what time do you want me to pick you up for hoops? I was thinking around quarter of one or so ..."

"Fuck that, I am not playing today ... My ankle is fucked up or something."

"Right, I'll pick you up at 12:45. No way am I showing up without you. We can't have just nine."

"Fine ... see ya then."

"Hold on—the real reason I am calling is to ask where you ended up after leaving the bar with—what's her name? Can you also shed some light on the cryptic text you sent to me at 4:07 in the morning?"

"Huh ..."

"Brian, go read your text and call me back after breakfast with Mom, because if we have to meet someone somewhere about whatever shit you somehow pulled us into last night, I have to start thinking of a story to get out of the house tonight. G ... Got it? Talk to you soon, buddy, and take some *Excedrin* for that hangover. B."

Immediately after hanging up with Chad, I scroll to find the message I wrote to him. It. Reads:

I forgot to tell you, we gotta do something, something later, later tonight. Call me, later.

Fuck. Fuck. Fuck. Fuck.

"Brian!"

"Mom!"

"What are you doing?"

Fuck. Fuck. Fuck.

"I'm coming, I'm coming! I'll be there in a minute! Drink your tea!"

"I didn't have to come. I can go back home. You're the one that called me ..."

She is at the bottom of the steps waiting for me, giving me the same stink eye she had when she walked in.

"See, Mom? I'm here, looking all pretty for you."

"Yes, dear, you're very handsome."

I peck her cheek and we walk out the door.

Breakfast is more of the same: her appraising, me deflecting. We bob and weave like Ali and Frazier, but now with eggs! She's not stupid and I'm not subtle, but we dance like this for a while before she finally just stares me in the eye and asks me what I want.

"Not much, Mom, just a little bit. Like eight hundred should do it... No, make it a thousand, yes. A thousand would be better. I swear I'll pay you back. You can even charge interest if you want—that's how sure I am I'll be able to pay you back."

"Honey, interest doesn't work if you don't *pay*. It's just a word then."

She doesn't believe me, which goes back to the whole not being stupid thing. She has no reason to believe me; I *am* lying ...

She gives me the money though. She even asks if I need it to be cash; her bank is open until noon on Saturdays. I'd be lying again if I said I didn't know that. Cash it was.

She dropped me off. It had been a long fucking morning, and it was all I could do to make it to the couch before passing out.

I wake with a sweaty start to Chad banging on my front door. The cable box says 12:40. I have got to make some changes in my life. Grownups sleep at appropriate times and wake up without all this noise and dread. At least until they have kids.

I never can get my head in the game. My jump shot is off and my ankle hurts. I miss layups I should make with my eyes closed and generally let Chad run circles around me. He runs his mouth the whole game, and I don't have the energy to fight back.

I don't get beers with the guys. I let Chad give me a hard time right up until he lets me off.

"Hey man, what am I supposed to tell my wife tonight? What are we doing?"

"Tell her whatever you want man, just meet me at the Old Freddie B's around eight and I'll explain everything."

"Alright, whatever, I'll see you there."

I close the door behind me. Poor Chad.

The sigh that escapes my lips is heavier than I intended, but appropriate for the next steps. It is 3:00 and there's a lot to do. It's time to get to work ...

I look around and notice the candle I lit this morning is still burning. "Great." I move to blow it out before the damn house burns to the ground. I walk into the kitchen looking for any remaining bottles of alcohol. I find a bottle of Tanqueray. That'll do. I grab orange juice and mix a drink to get the blood flowing.

I sit on the couch and while I have a moment of calm, I begin to piece together last night. A fight, some drugs, no money, lots of liquor, an ankle that's completely fucked, and a cryptic text message. Actually ... my ankle feels pretty horrific now that I'm thinking about it. I take my gin and juice, grab my wallet and keys, and head out the door.

Once I'm standing in the aisle at CVS looking for an ankle brace, I realize that tonight is just going to be a shit show of epic proportions. I feel as if I am gearing up for battle and if anyone sees that a 35-year-old man is wearing a goddamn ankle brace, I'll definitely get my ass kicked. Then I realize I have no idea why I'm even fighting someone.

As I get back home and open the door, my phone is ringing. It's Chad.

"Brian, I just remembered something from last night. Did you get in a fight with a drug dealer? Also I think you meant to hit him and ended up punching his girlfriend in the face."

I don't say anything.

"Oh well, I thought you should know. I'm still seeing you tonight at Freddie B's. I'm telling my wife you're having a mental breakdown and need moral support or some bullshit like that. I've got to go. The fucking kids want to go to the park ..."

I set the phone down. Goddamnit. I put the ankle brace on and down my drink to make another.

The doorbell rings. I realize I have fallen asleep. The clock on the DVD player says 7:26 P.M. I've got to meet Chad in less than an hour.

You have got to fucking be joking. I lie there on the couch and the doorbell keeps ringing.

I roll off the couch, blood rushing to my head, and squint my eyes shut to regain some clarity. I really need to get my life together. Maybe a 30-day detox? Ugh, even thinking about that sounds shitty.

I look out the window. It's Caroline, my ex-fiancé. God, she's hot. And I look like a drunken mess. I hope it's more charming and less total fuck-up.

Deep breath and I open the door.

She sighs ... "Well, it's good to see you're alive Brian ..."

"What are you talking about Caroline?" I say as I move aside to see if she wants to come in. She doesn't say anything, and she doesn't move from outside.

"Listen, you can come in if you want, but I have to go meet Chad at Freddie B's soon." I feel obligated to invite her too, even though I have no idea what kind of loose ends I'm going to have to embarrassingly tie up tonight.

"Feel free to, uh, come with us ..." I say, knowing all too well she will politely decline.

"Thank you, Brian, but I will have to take a rain check. Rachel, Sammy, and I are heading to Cary tonight for that surprise show I told you about."

"Oh yeah ... sounds fun." I mutter, never looking up from the floor to avoid eye contact with her. I find myself desperately wishing for an invite from Caroline to tag along. The urge to act on the temptation of heading out of town in order to avoid the impending encounter at Freddie B's continues for a few moments. The invitation never comes about, allowing for reality to settle back in.

"Just wanted to drop off your mail." She hands me three envelopes which appear to be past due bills and a catalog.

"I really need for you to change your mailing address this week. Can you put aside some time and do it?"

"Yeah ... I'll take care of it."

I finally looked up at her. She flashes that familiar cautious smile my way, walks back to her car, and drives away.

The clock in my car reads 8:34. I realize running slightly behind schedule has become the norm in my life. To kill off the thought of explaining my tardiness to Chad, I frantically push the scan button on my car stereo in search of a song to simply clear my head.

*XM*Channel 43 is where I land.

Thinkin' of a master plan/'Cuz ain't nuthin' but sweat inside my hand
So I dig into my pocket, all my money is spent
So I dig deeper but still comin' up with lint

"Fuck!" I scream in the confines of my car. I make a U-turn at the next light and speed back home.

I slam the car in park, remove the keys, and dart towards my front door. Walking through my front door, I see it instantly. There on the table, leaning up against the candle, is the bank envelope filled with the cash. I grab it and run back out, thanking Rakim for the reminder along the way.

The traffic lights on University Parkway are clearly not cooperating. The second consecutive red light leaves me visibly irate. Looking down at my phone, I see that a text from Chad, but before I can read it, the light flashes green. Since the traffic light gods are having their time with me, I stop following basic laws of the road. Approaching yet another traffic light, I correctly predict another red. This time I neglect to slow down. I push down on the gas and drive through the intersection as it turns red. I repeat this maneuver two more times before turning right on the street where the old Freddie B's resides.

Pulling into the dimly-lit, half-paved parking lot of the bar, I pick up the phone. Chad's text reads, 'I'm running late b there soon ... sorry.' The clock in my car reads 9:19. I pull into a spot but stay put in my car. I peer around to see if the handful of cars parked in the lot are any I recognize. My eye catches one jet black sports utility vehicle parked in a handicap spot that I instantly recognize. In fact, it's the same car I was dropped off in during the early hours of this morning. Knowing he is already here lets off an intense nervous feeling in the pit of my stomach.

Slouched in the driver's seat of my car, waiting on Chad, I reach into my jacket pocket and pull out the pack of cigarettes. I roll down the driver's side window about halfway and light a cigarette. Glancing out my window, I observe a steady flow of cars making their entrance into the parking lot. Chad's vehicle is still absent from the bunch. The age and appearance of the patrons entering the bar signals to me that a local blues band is playing here tonight. I begin to find myself thinking about Caroline and wondering what the topic of conversation is with her friends on their road trip. Just as the clock turns to 9:30, I have my moment of clarity.

I begin quickly filling the gaps from the night before with all the specific details that until now had lain dormant for much of the day. There were even a few times I chuckled at the absurdity of the situation that led me to sitting here at this precise moment. It was all there, presented chronologically in my mind: drinks at the bar with friends, the lack of judgment, the heightened sensitivity of those involved when alcohol and drugs are consumed in massive quantities, the argument, the failed negotiation, the thrown punch, being thrown down a flight of stairs, the reason for the text to Chad, the money owed but not had, and the twisting of my ankle on the steps leading to my bedroom.

Time to call Chad.

"I should be there in 10." Chad said, replacing the typical phone call pleasantry with details of his pending arrival.

"Chad, turn around and go home. Like always, I appreciate you making the effort. However, this time I think I have to clean this situation up myself."

"You sure?"

"I am. I'll give you a call tomorrow. I believe everything should work out."

"Alright ... call me if you need me though."

I thank him and hang up.

The bank envelope is nestled in the glove compartment. Resting underneath that very envelope is my 9mm. I turn off the car engine, stick the envelope of cash in my front pants pocket and the gun in the interior pocket of my winter jacket. I light one more cigarette and gather my thoughts into a plan for how this is all going to go down in the basement office of the bar.

It's 10:03 on my cell phone. I step out of the car and walk over to the front entrance to Freddie B's. One step through the door and the bouncer is requesting an ID. He briefly inspects my ID.

"You know where to go?"

I nod. He passes me through with a return of the nod. There was never a moment when I thought the bouncer would pat me down. Here at the old Freddie B's, it's always assumed you're carrying, including the staff.

I suddenly felt a boost of adrenaline kick in when passing through the emerging crowd of people settling in for a night of blues music and cheap draft beers. I continue on towards an inconspicuous corner of the bar which marks the entrance to the basement stairs. Pausing for a brief moment to inhale deeply, I push open the heavily-worn oak door leading to steps down into the basement. The first step of the stairs symbolizes the point of no return.

Oddly enough, as I make my way downward, I can no longer feel the nagging pain in my ankle.

YOU + ME = HELL
VICTORIA GRIFFIN

Our relationship is like a math problem, the kind that fills up pages of wide-ruled notebook paper. The kind no one ever solves.

$$1 + 1$$

We meet in the baby section at Wal-Mart. We're both buying presents for friends' baby showers. To her, that means we are destined to get married and have beautiful children together. To me, that means we both have pregnant friends.

I'm holding a pastel-colored article of clothing, which I could not accurately place on an infant's body—but I know it's labeled "newborn." She's gushing over socks barely big enough to cover my fingertips. She'll say later that our eyes locked, that there was instant chemistry. She'll insist angels sang, and the Earth reversed its rotation. I'll remember noticing the shape of her breasts through her cotton shirt. She's not wearing a bra.

$$1 + 1 + 0.5$$

We go on six dates before she invites me in. I take her to nice restaurants and smile a sucker's smile when she orders lobster risotto—even though she knows I'm an electronics salesman with enough debt to make the U. S. government cringe. I bring her flowers (plastic because she's allergic to everything) and listen as she rattles off names and gossip (yes, it's our fourth date—no, I don't remember her story about the oddly shaped mole on her second cousin's back).

She pretends not to be testing me, putting me through a series of challenges with a checklist in her hand before she deems me worthy of her sex (and I mean that in both of its applications).

I pretend I'm not tracing her nipples through that silken blouse, wondering why she chose not to wear a bra to dinner on a cool October night. I pretend I don't notice that two more of her buttons are undone since she returned from the bathroom, because that's what she wants. She wants me to notice those things—the lines of her cleavage, the way she swings her hips when she walks. That's why she does them: for me to notice and pretend I don't.

After dinner, I drive her back to her apartment. My hand-me-down Celica protests as I turn into the parking lot, and I try not to grumble as I walk her to the door. I kiss her goodnight and look into her eyes, wondering what her magic number is, wondering how many more times I'll have to listen to her stories about growing up in Florida, moving to Alabama, her golden retriever that died when she was twelve, her parents who never loved her enough (never bought her enough *stuff*), stories about things she remembers and things she's forgotten, people she loves and people she hates, places that move her and cities that should fall off the map, her clothes and her earrings and her *perfect* day at the outlets with her best friend she's known since she was negative three years old.

Just as I'm thinking I can't take any more (even when she's silent, I can't take anymore), she grips my coat with both hands and pulls herself into me like she's trying to hide in my skin. She kisses me harder than she has before, and she loops a thumb through my belt.

Then she says the words I've been waiting since date one to hear: "Do you want to come up for a drink?"

I don't even say, "yes," just reach around her to open the door. She leads the way.

She talks about drinks all the way up the stairs. She has a great bottle of wine, and didn't I say I liked whiskey? She has a brand new fifth of Jack Daniels and probably some Coke in the refrigerator if that's how I drink it. I mumble something about drinking it straight, but it doesn't matter because as soon as we step through the doorway she's reaching up to kiss me like a giraffe stretching for high leaves. Our coats hit the floor—two mounds of heavy, black fabric like placeholders for us—as we scamper into her bedroom. She peels off her dress and slips her body around me. I barely see her skin. The lights are off, the room lit only by streetlights and headlights gliding through the window. I feel the waves of her spine and the heavy flesh of her thighs. I feel her wispy hair fall onto my chest. I feel her want me.

My mind is fuzzy from the drink I didn't have. The sex isn't great, but whoever said sex is like pizza was dead on. Even a bad one's still pretty damn good.

Or it would have been.

A week later she calls me. We haven't spoken since that night. I thought it was odd. Usually after sex, women get clingy to the nth degree. But I hadn't heard anything, not even a text. I called her once and left a voicemail. Three days later, I'm about to write off the whole thing (one good night, can't complain) when my phone rings.

She doesn't even say hello.

"I'm pregnant."

$$1 + 1 + 0.5 - 9,000$$

I think I'll shoot myself today. It's a common thought for me now. *I'll grab a burger for lunch, pick up eggs from the store, then take my old .45 and blow my fucking brains against the wall.*

When this particular desire for self-destruction hits me—along with the nausea, which has become as frequent as bowel movements—I'm standing in front of a glass case glittering with diamonds.

"I am supposed to spend *how much?*"

The salesman is perfectly rigid. He looks like his face has been pressed along with his tie. "Three months' salary is the accepted—"

"I don't know whether that bullshit was dropped by the diamond corporations or women, but I'm sure they both latched onto it like it was made of fucking sugar."

"Sir, if you would like a less extravagant ring for this—*lucky* lady, I can certainly—"

"Yeah, less *extravagant.* I want some dime store jewelry. I'm talking Cracker Jack prize. Got anything like that?"

The salesman grimaces (actually *grimaces*) and folds his manicured fingers on top of the case. "I'm afraid not. May I suggest the prize machines in the food court?"

I wink at him and walk out, my little bit of dignity stuck like gum to the bottom of my shoe. I think I'll leave it there awhile.

Back at my apartment (it'll be *our* apartment soon), a quick online search finds *Genuine DIAMOND Ring!* Twenty dollars.

Your purchase will arrive in 5-7 business days.

$$1 + 1 + 0.5 - 9{,}000 - 50{,}000$$

We've been married five years. Little Dani (full name: Danica, after Danica Patrick—my wife had never heard of her and thought it was just the *cutest name*) is about to start kindergarten. I never dreamed that I could be this complacent, this still, this—content? No, I wouldn't go that far.

Sometimes, though, when Dani and I are alone, I would even say I'm happy. It's a strong word, but when we walk across town to buy smoothies or go up to the roof right before bedtime, pretending to see shooting stars and making up constellations, there's no other word to describe it.

But now we're moving. Soon. Per order of the queen bee.

My Atlanta apartment, the one that was "the *perfect* place to raise a child!" is now cramped and old-fashioned. Too much in the city—and too near everything I love, presumably.

So it's time to move to a nice place in a good neighborhood where we can build decks and remodel two-year-old kitchens. It's time to shell out fifty grand to watch the remains of my life spin down a slow-flushing toilet.

And then the toilet will clog, and I'll have to fix it. Because who the fuck has money to call a plumber?

If it weren't for Dani, I would kill myself. Not because I won't get to see the Braves play their opening game or because I'll be cut off from my friends—the only real family I've ever had after my parents died. No, I would kill myself because of *her*.

Really, it's my wife I want to kill. Every time she oozes over me in bed, every time she opens her heinous mouth, filled only with selfish words, every time she tells me something else she *needs*, she *has to have*, every time I walk into that goddamn office building because "a corporate sales rep makes *so much more money* than an electronics salesman," I want to strangle her.

But suicide is simpler than murder. I long for it, think about it when I'm driving my shitty little Celica. Would it hurt too badly to swerve into that tree? What about off the bridge? I could put an empty bottle in the passenger seat and make it look like a drunken accident—to save face, to spare Dani.

Dani ... Who would have thought the thing that ruined me would be the only thing keeping me alive?

$$1 + 1 + 0.5 - 9{,}000 - 50{,}000 / 2$$

I wonder which part of Dani I get to keep. I need the right arm—the girl has a nasty curve—and the mouth so I can hear all her jokes, and I couldn't live without those desperately sweet hazel eyes. Her mother can have her hair. She can glue it onto a mannequin and dress it up, pretend its Dani. That's all our daughter is to her anyway. A dress-up doll. Buy her pearls, braid her hair—*Awe, how pretty! No, be quiet, honey. Dolls aren't supposed to speak.*

I saw my lawyer yesterday—told my wife I was working late. She thinks I'm cheating on her. No, thank God I never have. I can say that honestly. I think I knew that when the time came to divorce this bitch she would find every one of my indiscretions, and that was one bit of leverage I refused to give her.

Still, the courts almost always side with the mother. That's what my lawyer told me. We're doing our best to be prepared before I file for divorce so I at least have a chance to keep Dani. Eight years ago, I would never have thought I could feel this way. I would have laughed at the idea that money—*my* money, now stuck in fashionable stocks and appliances and outdoor renovations and my wife's fifteen million pairs of shoes—would mean nothing to me. I don't care. She can have it.

That's all she wants, after all. The money. She spends half her life complaining: "Can't we hire some *help*? A *nanny*? A *maid*? A *cook*?" Like she has better things to do. Like raising (I use the term loosely) our daughter is cutting into her hair salon/manicure/tanning time. The woman spends all day primping but only gets uglier.

Can't cover up that heart.

$$1 + 0.5 + 9,000 + 50,000 / 2 + 0$$

I finally understand what it means to fight *tooth and nail*. I bit and scratched and tore at every loose thread I could find, but I was the only thing that unraveled.

The judge doesn't care that she was a shitty wife or a shitty mother. He doesn't care that she all but hates her daughter or that she treats me like a golden chicken—only good until it stops laying eggs, then you break its neck and serve it for dinner. Apparently her sheer possession of a uterus makes her more qualified than I to raise our daughter.

When the judge awards her full custody, I spit at him. Not on him, just in his general direction. A night in jail for contempt of court tops off her case against me like the last bit of gas into the tank.

Apparently I have a drinking problem, a pornography addiction, and intimacy issues. I wasn't aware that my *two* beers on Sunday afternoons constitute alcoholism or that jacking off once in a while (it's not like I got what I needed from my cold-ass wife) makes me a pervert. I can barely hear with my heart working overtime, driving my blood pressure higher than her lunacy, but I'm pretty sure she mentioned my dick not working.

Really, who could get it up for her?

I hear myself crying in the hotel shower, sickeningly warm water dripping over me, without enough pressure to rinse the suds from my buzzed hair. It doesn't sound real, the sound of sobs bellowing from my stomach. I sound like an amateur actor trying to fake tears, not knowing how, settling for something between crying and screaming.

But it is real. It's all real. Jesus, it hurts.

you + 0.5 + 9,000 + 50,000 / me – everything = fuck it

I sell my car and buy an old truck off Craigslist. The air's broken, but the windows crank down, the warm breeze keeping the temperature just bearable. The wind licks Dani's hair as she licks her ice cream cone. It's melting all over her hands. I tell her to toss it out—I'll buy her another one. She crunches down on the cone one good time before chucking it at a stop sign. The vanilla ice cream hits just above the O, dripping slowly down the red sign and following the cone into the grass. *That's my girl.*

We'll be in Canada in a few days. I can count them on one hand.

But then, I've done enough counting. The only numbers I want to worry about now are Dani's birthdays. I hope they go slowly, but I know they won't.

My daughter has her feet propped on the dash. Her mother would have smacked her for that. I reach over and flick one of her pretty, dark curls into her eyes. She swats it away like a mosquito and laughs. There is excitement in her laugh, spewing from her little frame—we're going on an adventure.

She'll grow up faster than I could ever imagine, and maybe she'll resent me for taking her away from her mother, picking her up from school with a loaded truck and a bottle of Yoo-hoo in the passenger seat. But she would have resented me more for leaving her there.

Then again, maybe not. Maybe I'm not doing this for her, but for me. When it came down to it, I had two choices: live in Canada, with Dani, or die alone in America. I chose to live. For at least ten more years, I will choose to live. After that, I make no promises. When it's back to

1

I may not be able to stay here. I don't know if I can work this math problem again.

THE DIVINE TRILOGY
CRAIG HARTGLASS

One

"I had another dream. They were laughing at me."

"Who?"

"All of them. It's always the same."

"How did that make you feel?"

"I woke in a sweat, heart pounding. I couldn't get back to sleep. They were all there, my father, my younger brother. My oldest brother was lording over the proceedings."

"Like a roast?"

"They take turns at the lectern, mocking me. My failures. My oldest brother—don't get me started on him: square shoulders, perfect hairline—my oldest brother playing emcee, and I know he loves it, loves berating me in front of my father, my whole family, friends, colleagues. My cousins laugh. All of them laugh. Why not? They've managed to create worlds whose inhabitants get along, who aren't selfish, don't destroy everything they touch, everything given to them. Who are actually grateful. Kind to each other! I don't know why I say it like it's such a shock. Mine is the only place where they're so deplorable. Humans—who knew?!"

"Inside, outside."

"Huh?"

"You're judging their outsides from your inside. It's a distortion, an illusion."

"No, it's not! I'm a failure. These humans hate each other and kill each other and can't get along. They kill other creatures indiscriminately, sometimes out of spite. You ever heard of buffalos? —great furry beasts; horns, hooves, placid as rainwater? —anyway the humans take these buffaloes and guess what they do? They circle around them, yelling, screaming, sounding terrifying yelps—chaos! —in order to get the herd crazy, riled up, provoking them until a stampede breaks out, thousands of buffalo charging in fear... And you know what they do then, these humans, hallmark of my creation? They run them off a cliff... So they fall to their deaths, a giant crushed pile! The meat rots! Thousands of dead rotting buffalo. And do you know why they do this? Because some other group of humans, their enemies, depend on buffalo meat for sustenance. So they run them off cliffs! Seriously! And I created this. How could I not have seen it coming?"

"I think you're being hard on yourself. We've talked about this."

"I know what you're saying, but at some point you've got to face facts. Take responsibility. Don't you always say that, 'take responsibility'?"

"Yes. But I think you understand that this is different."

"It's not different. I'm a failure. On my brother's planet, I'll give you an example, do you know what they do on my brother's planet? No? They gather together, the different tribes, hand-in-hand, singing—"

"That's nice. But let's get back to your dream."

"The dream. Okay. So my cousin gets up there, on the dais, and he starts with, 'Natural selection—how's that working out? Y'all know about natural selection, don't you? That's where one animal eats another, who then eats another, so the ones with the strongest, sneakiest, most devious tendencies get to pass on their genes—and here everyone looks at one another, and you can see they're trying not to laugh, trying to keep it together, but the ludicrousness, the insanity of this scheme hits them, and one by one little squeaks come out—squeaks they try to hold back, but can't—and soon everyone is roaring, the entire room, and you can see the whole evolution concept playing out behind their eyes. I mean, setting up a system that rewards the basest characteristics, selfishness, greed, brutality, then keeping your hands off and expecting anything else to happen, expecting the experiment to go any other way, would be crazy. Right? So they're laughing, and I am sinking into a pit: humiliation, despair, burning shame—how could I not have anticipated it? How could I have been so stupid? So naïve?!Of course, I pretend to go along with them— 'Ha ha ha ha ha,' I say—laughing along, so funny! But inside I want to kill my cousin, tear his stupid face off, rip him to shreds, and my brother, too ... my brother who's egging him on, while my father sits there, watching, judging with those all-seeing eyes of his, and of course he knows what I'm thinking, what I'm feeling, all of it, my intentions—yet he never sees my brother's cruelty, never sees how he picks and picks and berates ... oh no, not him, not the golden boy! And I sink deeper into this pit, and my cousin, Mr. Jokeman, now he starts to illustrate it, using my humans, probably the worst example—or the best, I suppose, depending on perspective—and he says, and I'm paraphrasing here, he says, after five-thousand generations, this evolution, this 'intelligent design,' and he says this last part in a derisive tone, mocking, the way a wife of thirty years might say 'What a brilliant idea!' to her failure of a husband after listening to yet another of his get-rich-quick ideas; and he, my cousin, says, in this mocking tone, 'This intelligent design has selected for the meanest, cruelest, most vicious creatures imaginable,' before going on to list some of their finer moments, their grandest atrocities, as well as the everyday ones, the imaginary borders and rules and tales set forth as justification to slaughter one another, an activity they love beyond measure, down to their deepest cells—though they pretend otherwise—not to mention the double-dealing in ordinary transactions, or the way they treat other animals over whom they've given themselves stewardship ... raising them in giant camps so that if their intention had been to make these creatures' every waking minute as torturously unpleasant as possible they couldn't have done any better... but now, he says, my cousin, pausing to allow the gravity of what he is about to say sink in—and it works, because the laughter dies and slowly the mood turns from mocking to grim (not just grim, but grim and accusatory). And: NO! I'm not imagining it! And he says that they, these humans, have developed a new means of slaughtering one another, and 'It's ingenious,' he says, 'so clever and efficient that if I were their leader I'd have no choice but use it, despite the blaring immorality of the thing.' And here he shakes his head, his face expressing horror and disgust, before saying, 'They've developed contraptions that soar through the sky, silent as birds, nearly undetectable, and these contraptions shoot people and buildings and drop bombs, while their operators—the new warriors!—are hundreds of miles away, thousands of miles away—sealed in climate-controlled buildings and staring at screens while operating keyboards and handsets, like some sort of game, snacking on chips, sipping cola—foods, I might add,' he chuckles, 'engineered to minimize health and longevity and maximize momentary glutinous pleasure—so opposing soldiers never meet face to face; the horror of battle is eliminated, but also the nobility and valor, which, as brutal as warfare is, you have to admit, is there, that valor—but now they kill without witnessing death or blood, without hearing the screams of the fallen; no torn up flesh, no body parts sailing through the air, no crying, anguished loved ones—and the most tragic part, the most ironic, heartbreaking part, is that the stress of this, this war without warfare, is that so many soldiers go mad over time and end up killing themselves with drugs or liquor, sometimes directly with their weapons—and they die anyway! It's true,' my cousin adds, with a smirk I want to punch through his face so it comes out the other side. But of course I can't say anything. I can't defend myself. I can't tell them what my intentions were. And my father's sitting there, downing gin and tonics, probably on his eighth, everyone so merry ..."

"What were your intentions? What would you tell them if you could?"

"I thought I'd make the whole thing self-sustaining. From the tiniest bacteria to the hugest whale, a complex network of dependency. Nobody had done that before. That's what I wanted. That's what I was shooting for. The idea was ingenious! Elegant! Each piece contingent on the actions of the others, a perfect balance ... I imagined myself winning awards, accepting accolades from peers, going down in the history books. But it failed. It's a failed experiment. So what do I do? Wreck the thing and start over?"

"What do you think you should do?"

"I think—"

"Whoa, look at the clock!"

"But I haven't gotten to—"

"Why don't we save that for next week."

Two

The memo hit His office at four o'clock, a Friday afternoon. Jason, His young assistant, on his way out the door, stopped to switch the widescreen on the wall back on. He keyed in the code from the memo. He saw the bees.

It was an emergency meeting of Local 124. Jason was watching, *Honeybees; Drones and Workers*, and they had grievances. They were tired of being medicated, boxed and trucked thousands of miles, put to work pollinating tons of a single crop, almonds, tulips, bosc pears, apricots, whatever. Tired of the workload, the bad food, the lack of variety. They were ready to strike. "I mean, they send us all the way to California and we don't even get to see Disney," whispered one bee to her friend.

"I know! Or that Chinese Theatre."

"I want to see John Wayne's footprints, where Lucy—"

"ORDER!" The queen sat up front at the head of a long table, flanked by two underlings who were filling her nectar glass and massaging her wings. She smacked the gavel and the roar quieted. "COME TO ORDER!!!"

In attendance were reps, delegates, a smattering of the rank and file. Because there were no longer sufficient numbers of honeybees to keep up with pollination, the queen said, she had requested assistance from wasps, hornets, bumblebees, and various other flying pollinators. She'd said things were grave, that her population was dwindling, something in the crops making them sick, killing them off.

A honeybee in the middle row stood and shouted, "I hate that new stuff! It tastes terrible!"

"Tastes terrible?" said another. "I'm on the toilet sixteen times a day. My belly is a gurgling whirlpool!"

"I'm allergic to ragweed now!"

"My son has asthma!"

This prompted mutters about cutbacks to the health plan (due to spiraling costs), and the lousy coverage, which in turn led to rumors of bankruptcy and foreclosure, followed by hive collapse. Nods. Shouts. "Enough is enough!!"

Jason picked up the telephone. "Boss, we got trouble."

"I was going to play a quick nine before dinner," the Big Boss said, swallowing the last of His martini before straightening the collar on His golf shirt. "They're about to call me to tee—"

"It's a crisis."

"Okay," the Big Boss said, "what's the problem?" He had returned to the office and was setting up a line of golf balls on the carpet with the tip of His putter. He tapped one. It veered left, a mile off of the cup. "Damn!" He said.

Jason pointed to the widescreen, told Him about the bees.

"What's the big deal? Let them strike."

"The ecological balance of the planet depends on bees, Sir."

"How can that be? They're so tiny!"

"It comes down to microbes."

"Microbes? What? Like bacteria?"

Jason nodded. He explained that bacteria grew in the guts and mucus membranes of the bees, in all His creatures really, and that these microbes were responsible for maintaining health, vitality, and good spirits, and for regulating immunity. If they fed the microbes the right stuff, Jason continued, stuff that His Father's Father had laid out perfectly, they go to work fighting illness, thinking happy, positive thoughts. But if they didn't, it would all go to hell. "Bees need a variety of flowering plants, thousands a day, to maintain their diversity of microbes. And the humans give them one."

"One?" The Boss was distracted. Between putts, He'd grabbed the clicker and was now trying to change the channel. When it didn't work He pressed the button harder, karate chopping his arm in the direction of the screen. "How the hell do you work this thing?"

Jason pointed out the button with the arrow.

"Ahh," the Boss said. He switched the widescreen from the bees to a basketball game. "Listen, Irwin," He said into the telephone, "I need to double my action on Oklahoma State. Yeah, yeah, all of it."

"About the bees," Jason said. "The humans give them one plants a day for weeks on end."

Just then, old Ginny, His secretary, shuffled in. Ginny had been running the office since the beginning. She'd been His Father's secretary, and His Father's before that. Compared to them, she thought, He was lazy and entitled: a dilettante and absentee landlord running the enterprise into the ground. "The flounder is on the line, Sir," she said.

"Flounder?" The Boss shook his head. He stepped to the bar and poured a martini from His crystal pitcher before lighting a cigar. He ran a fingertip over the surface of the pitcher, parting the cool beads of sweat. "That's a fish, right?"

"Yes, Sir," Ginny said.

In the last decade, at the greedy hands of the humans, the flounder and cod populations had dropped off. Now they were always going on about genocide. It was tedious. The last time He put them through, He'd gotten an earful. "The ocean floor is coated in petroleum!" the flounder had whined. "Everyone is sick! Males are being born with no nuts! Females with three of 'em!"

Or had that been the frogs? Or starfish? Who could keep it straight?

"Ginny, tell them we're on it." He winked, then sipped His martini and switched the screen to a football game. "Throw the damn ball, you idiot!" He hollered, reaching for the phone. "Irwin, what do I owe? Total? Okay, give me Detroit and the under!"

"Sir, about the bees," Jason said. "If bees die out, plants won't get pollinated, and if plants don't get pollinated, vast swaths of plant species will be wiped out, and if vast swaths of plant species are wiped out, vast swaths of animal species will follow, until nothing is left but weeds, then nothing at all."

"And this is because of microbes."

"At root, Sir. Yes."

"And it's the humans?"

Jason nodded.

"Ginny! Get the humans on the line!" He pointed to Jason, "You talk to them, Jay-Jay."

Jason explained the situation to the humans.

"Our position," the humans replied, "is that none of this is our fault. Animals go extinct all the time."

"Who do they think they're talking to?" the Big Boss fumed.

Jason put his hand over the mouthpiece. "They say to tell you that the humans have been behaving responsibly. It's not their fault if the animals are too weak to withstand environmental changes."

"Maybe they should have been designed better," the humans said, loud enough to carry across the room, "besides—it's in our lease!"

"Lease?"

"Right there," Jason said, pointing out verse and line that described, "... Dominion over the fish of the sea and over the birds of the heavens and over the Earth and over every creeping thing that creeps over the Earth."

The Boss rubbed his eyes. "Is that it?"

Jason put a palm over the phone again. "They called you a tree hugger, Sir."

"What is that?"

"The ones with dirty clothes and no jobs, I think."

"I hate those fuckers!"

"Sir, your father used to—"

"I'm running things, not my father! Ginny!" He roared, "Put together an explanatory press release for humankind, a warning call." He poured another martini and drank it and poured another and drank it and poured one more.

Jason switched from the football game. The bees came back on.

"In closing," the Queen was saying, "I'm calling on the noblesse of members and allies: Bee, Wasp, Hornet," on her feet now, scepter raised, "We must stand together in this hour of need, and take responsibility..."

"Why do we have to pick up the slack?" yelled an angry wasp.

"It's not fair!" snarled a hornet.

Ginny shuffled back into the office. "Sir, the humans are on line one responding to the press release."

The press release had explained that the situation was dire. If things continued as they were going, it said, the future of life on the planet, from plant to primate, including humans, was grim. Everything would die. It went on to say that He had given them all that was needed for remediation. He had laid it out. They were to stop tampering with His designs, and they were to leave the bees alone, free to do their work, to pollinate at will. And slowly the planet would recover. Life would continue.

"Sorry, that won't work for us," the humans said.

"Look, that stuff you're putting in the crops to kill weeds and bugs is killing the bees, killing the microbes in their guts, microbes they need ... It's wrecking their immune systems, their nervous systems!"

"We're willing to compromise."

Jason closed his eyes, ran a hand through his hair. His mouth was suddenly dry. "Compromise?"

"Warning labels."

"The bees are dying! The planet is dying!"

"That's just a theory," the humans said.

"It's not a theory. Take a headcount! You're dying too."

"Too much meat?" the humans said. "How about we draw a picture of a dinner plate, and cover a third with rhubarb?"

Jason stared at the phone.

"A pyramid?" the humans said.

There was a lull, a delicious quiet. Jason felt himself yielding, a drowning man letting go, taking that final sleepy breath. Then, from the widescreen, a cacophony of angry voices sounded at once. Startled, they all looked up.

"No way!" A defiant hornet was shaking his fist. "I'm not going to do it."

"Me neither!" said another, turning and marching out.

"STRIKE!! STRIKE!!"

The remainder of the wasps, hornets, bumblebees, and various flying pollinators followed. One by one, the honey-bee rank and file filed out, too, until all that was left were the delegates. Then they walked out, too, followed by the Queen's underlings. She stood alone, behind her table, in the silent, empty hall.

"Irwin," The Big Boss cradled the phone to his shoulder as he lined up a long, straight shot with his putter. He tapped the ball and watched it roll slowly to the cup before dropping in with a clatter. He gulped His martini and puffed His cigar. "Irwin," He finally said, exhaling a narrow band of smoke, "Give me the line on Earth ..."

Three

On the night of December fourteenth at ten P.M., exactly two hours and ten days before Christmas (and, coincidentally, his thirty-third birthday), Russell Black, divorced, unemployed, nearly friendless, suffering a skin condition of unknown etiology, that, due to incapacitating shame fueled by social anxiety, demanded long sleeves in the height of summer (certainly no swimwear!), stood before his bathroom mirror with the barrel of a nine-millimeter pistol pressed to his temple. This was no rash decision. He had been thinking about it a long time. After nearly thirty-three years walking this planet, he had come to the realization that what was widely held up as good, all that was idealized and sought after, was in fact evil. That the truths of men, their guiding principles, the values and promises held closest to their hearts, were nothing but fictions designed to perpetuate the power of those who held it and keep it at arm's length, like a carrot before a burdened donkey, from those who didn't. In most instances, these truths were outright lies. He saw that any person who tried to lead a kind, decent, moral life was, for his efforts, crushed into dust.

What kind of world was that? Who would want to live in such a place?

"Who indeed," came a quiet voice of retort in his head.

Russell paid the voice no mind. He was a man of deep thought and philosophical leanings, and consequently, engaged in these sorts of internal back-and-forths routinely. As he prepared breakfast, washed dishes, or cut the grass, for example, it was not uncommon to play out an internal dialog, Socratic in nature, regarding anything from the existence of God (unlikely), to the availability of affordable housing for the sick and elderly in a fair-and-open market (assuming there was such a thing). Therefore, when met with this voice, he attributed its presence to an inner sparring partner, one of a stable of players who inhabited his subconscious, like a chorus of backup singers dutifully serving up the time-honored response to his reverential call.

In his mind, Russell continued to make his case. He listed events of unthinkable barbarism perpetrated by humanity—torture, genocide, the polar bears—as well as acts of callousness and double dealing, small-minded cruelties played out daily on countless smaller stages by his brothers and sisters: lies, deception, manipulation, the flimflam that was, so far as he could tell, the currency of human interaction. Even the animal kingdom, he lamented, as the cool barrel trembled and warmed to his temple, was rife with brutality. There were reptiles he'd seen on television that ripped small mammals into pieces, and over a period of hours, as their victims' dying mammalian hearts pumped and lungs wheezed, and as their furry little eyes stared through a film of terror and helplessness, the bloodless reptiles devoured them, organ by limb, while still alive!

"What about it?" the voice said.

"What about it? "What about it?!" This second time, Russell spoke out loud, aiming the outburst at his own reflection. "What kind of world is that? What kind of God would allow such a place? Would create it?" He went on to describe beasts that inject into their prey a venom that keeps them alive but paralyzed while the predator's eggs, just laid, mature and hatch into a squirming gelatin of larvae that feasts on the doomed, but living and aware, creature's insides. "Who would want to live in such a place? What kind of sick mind would design it? Why?"

These last words Russell shouted, his voice shaking.

"What kind of design? Ha!!What kind do you think?"

He heard the words again in his mind. But now the voice was foreign, and the words seemed to appear from nowhere, with no connection to himself. The normal human process that moves from thought to word-search to sentence assembly, quietly occurring in one's head, had been bypassed. The words simply appeared.

"Who are you?" Russell demanded.

"Who do you think, Russell?"

"How do you know my name?"

"Look, kid, I'm in your head—don't you think I'd know your name?"

Russell stared at his reflection. While he'd never been much of a looker, no movie star certainly, he'd always appeared clear-eyed and healthy. But now he had that colorlessness of flesh and wildness of eye that in television movies was the precursor to insanity. He stepped back.

"Am I losing my mind?" he whispered.

"Hardly." The voice laughed. "You're more sane than most."

The irony of a man standing before his bathroom mirror with a gun at his head being called "more sane than most" by an unrecognizable voice that may or may not be originating in his own head was not lost on Russell. "Who are you?" he said.

"Exactly who you think."

There followed a back and forth of disbelief and assurance, until at Russell's behest, an image appeared in the mirror. It was terrifying! A vast swirling entity of color and light, smoke and vapor; it crashed thunder and sparked lightning and raged like a thousand angry seas, all while emanating a golden radiance of wisdom, mastery, authority, judgment, and power.

Russell jumped back. He screamed.

"I know," the voice said. "I get that a lot."

"It's just that I was expecting…"

"George Burns?" A chuckle. Then the image transformed from the twisting, swirling haze into that comforting old man, robed, bearded, sandal-wearing, of myth and legend. "Better?"

Russell stared, nodded.

As the startle cleared, Russell felt calm, more than situation or reason would dictate. "I don't get it," he whispered. "I mean, why would you go through the trouble of creating all this," he spread his arms as he'd seen television preachers do to suggest all of creation, "then make everyone so foolish and greedy, their interactions cruel, crooked, corrupt, filled with avarice and …" Russell paused, "well, just bad stuff?" he said.

"Ah … Yes, that *is* the question, isn't it? Why do you think?"

"How would I know?"

"You're the one with the gun at your head. That would indicate you've given it some thought."

"Wouldn't it indicate that the whole thing is beyond my comprehension?"

"Maybe you comprehend more than you think. You've always been hard on yourself. One of those weight-of-the-world types."

"I might have guessed." Russell shook his head. He chuckled. "With nature's indifference, and men the way they are …"

"Yeah, yeah."

"And created in your image, no less."

"Whoa! I never said that. That whole 'in-his-own-image' thing—that didn't come from me!"

"Do you like looking down—or however you do it—on this mess?"

"I have hope."

"Hope? Then you're a fool."

"Maybe."

Russell thought a moment. "What about all the preachers?" he said.

The bearded one shook his head. "Don't get me started."

"The Ten Commandments?"

"Good. But not from me."

"So there's no truth to the big three... Judaism, Christianity, Islam?"

"Nope."

"I knew it."

"Do you really think I'd make a guy drag his kid up a volcano—"

"It was a mountain."

"There are lots of versions. Do you think I'd have him drag the kid up a volca—, up a mountain, then raise a knife overhead, awaiting my command to plunge the weapon into the boy's heart?"

Russell made a weighing of hands. "Seems about right," he said.

"So I'm omniscient, omnipotent, wise, powerful, all knowing? ... filled with love and forgiveness, yet petty and childish enough to behave like the worst of the worst of you?"

Russell shrugged. "So there's no heaven?" he said.

"Oh, there *is* a heaven."

"Then the religions are right?"

"That part they got right, I hate to admit."

"I don't understand," Russell said. He stared off. "You know, when I was in junior high there was a kid who chased a retarded boy down the hall with lit matches." After a pause, he went on to say that the retarded boy, a tall, slender, lamb of a child, was terrified of fire, and somehow this other boy recognized his weakness and would light matches and hold them up to his face, then chase him. "He'd light one after another, while Jimmy, the retarded one, ran screaming down the hallway, trying to escape."

"Horrible."

"Horrible? Is that all you've got? Jimmy, this retarded lamb, would scream 'FIRE!!' over and over as he ran, his voice a crying bleat. Terrified. It was like Frankenstein running from the villagers. Worse! He had a flatfooted gait, and as he ran you'd hear his shoe soles—penny loafers! —slapping the tile floor. And Frankie, the one with the matches, and later a cigarette lighter—which I wonder if he brought especially for this purpose, or if it was a happy coincidence? —and Frankie would be laughing as he chased behind. We watched, but no one stopped him. I didn't do anything. I was scared. The first time I saw it I felt like I was going to throw up. 'FIRE!' That voice is with me to this day. Why did you allow that?"

The figure shrugged.

Russell waved the gun before his face, looked at it a moment, then put it back to his temple. "There was another kid in that school," he said. "He wore a wig. No hair, no eyebrows, no body hair. Can you imagine how that must have been? Junior high, no hair! As if that's not enough, one day another kid sneaks behind him and knocks off the wig. It was lunchtime, a beautiful sunny day, kids laying back on the grassy hillside, munching cookies, sandwiches, chips, sipping milk through straws, when this other kid, another bully, sneaks behind him and knocks the wig off his head with a stick and yells for everyone to look. Then, when the hairless kid, red-faced and crying now, lunges for the wig, the bully kicks it away. Everyone laughed and pointed." Russell shook his head. "Excuse me if I don't hold you in the highest esteem."

"What do you want me to tell you? That it's not fair? That it can't be?"

"Why not? You're in charge, why can't it be?"

"If it were intended to be fair, childhood would come at the end, after a long life, once experience has beaten away idealism."

"Great! Profound! You know, I read that book, too."

"Good, right?"

"I liked his first better; with the neurotic guy and the college girlfriend."

The figure nodded. "That *was* better. I forgot that one."

Russell stared. "The innocence of children—what they're forced to learn, the way they're forced to learn it: the ultimate cruelty. Maybe your best work!"

"You were picked on yourself, weren't you? Shamed, beaten, made to feel small, weak, stupid. Isn't that right?"

Russell nodded.

"And what did you do when you had the chance? Did you become Gandhi, Sister Theresa—a righter of wrongs, friend to the weak and voiceless? Did you become the hero of your imagination?"

Russell felt his face reddening.

"No. You perpetuated the same cruelty you lived through. You want to talk about junior high, Russell? Remember that boy in art class, the scrawny one with the bad clothes and a girl's name? What was it?"

Russell looked down, mumbled, "Evelyn."

"Yes, Evelyn. Remember what happened?"

"I teased him."

"Teased him?!Surely you remember better than that. You had gotten stronger, and as a consequence there was another boy in that class, Roland, who sat beside you, who looked up to you, idolized you even. And how did you behave? You, a boy who had been picked on, teased, beaten and mocked?"

Russell bowed his head. "I showed off for Roland."

"Showed off? You were so cruel that eventually this hapless boy, Evelyn, your victim, went into a frenzy, attacked you."

"I was a monster. He threw a stapler at me."

"And then what happened?"

"I was frightened."

"Besides that?"

"I was made humble. Human. It was like a window opened, a portal back to my humanity. In that moment, I was the bully. I saw that I'd pushed this kid to the point of breaking, I saw his spirit flattened, his heart crying. I felt sick. Diseased. But, you know, even while I was acting out I felt bad—I mean, I felt good too, powerful—but bad, like I knew it was a sickness. Still, I couldn't stop myself. When it reached the boiling point, when he was forced to react and confront me, I drew back. I saw what I'd done: I'd turned into everything I despised. I was hiding behind this new person I had become, this newly invented identity, one who wasn't going to be pushed, abused ... but now, suddenly, that old me was back—and I realized it was the best of me: empathetic, fully human."

"This realization, did it last?"

Russell shook his head. "No."

"You did the same with your mother, your wife. Anyone who loved you."

"Yes."

"Why?"

"I don't know," Russell said.

"Don't you think there's a purpose to all of it? I mean, do you think this whole setup, this elaborate interplay of life and energy, thought, matter, and emotion, the confluence of intention and deed, for which you have so painfully dashed me, yourself, and all of creation, over the rocks... do you think that what you're recognizing, the faults, evils, double-dealing, has a purpose...? Other than fodder for daytime programming, I mean?"

Silence.

"Think, man... Think!!"

"The purpose?" Russell said. "You're impossibly cruel. A sadist! The lowest of low. Letting children die while men fatten their pockets with the profits of pilfered supplies! Disease! Famine! Pain! Don't let's get started on pain. We're born in pain and all the way through is nothing but pain. So much pain we invent escapes, means of anesthetization, deluding ourselves with drugs and drink, food and thrills, living through others—children, lovers, TV stars, politicians—soul-deadening perversions, mindless numbing sex, material acquisition, our souls aching so badly our skin hurts... All this excess, and why?—so that for a few minutes, the pain of our crappy existence is numbed... Not even numbed, wall-papered over, still there but buried so deep that, though you feel it, sense it, for a few minutes you can't see it. We need an imagination with crazy ability to conjure nonsense just to get through a fucking day, let alone the string of them that make up a miserable life."

"Bravo! But why?"

"You tell me!"

"Come on, Russell. There's got to be a point."

"What kind of point can there be?"

"You think you're the first to see this, to realize it?"

"A test?"

The question, Russell suddenly came to understand, wasn't: 'Who could create such a place?' No, the question was: 'Who could live in it?' With the daily insults to virtue, the compromises to integrity, the moral and philosophical codes necessarily ignored to get by in society—lies, corruption, evil—not to mention the self-weakness and cowardice that show in those key moments when we expect to see strength. Who could live in such a place? Or maybe, it then struck Russell, the question was: '*Who couldn't?*'

For whom would it be too much? For whom would it be impossible?

"It would be impossible for the good," Russell whispered. "The truly good."

"Yes!"

"For the decent, the righteous, the kind. For the innocent it would be unbearable. It would break their hearts, their spirits." At once it came to him, a rush of insight. "They would have to kill themselves."

"Heaven is for the righteous, Russell."

In that second the meaning of existence became clear to Russell: pain, struggle, loss, all of it. As he squeezed the trigger, he heard the voice again, but now it was tender, loving, its velvety tones imbued with a warmth that enveloped him, a wome glow he instinctively recognized as home. He closed his eyes and let the voice wash over him.

"Welcome," it said.

CAN'T FALL DOWN
LESLIE BOHEM

Alex got out of the car on First Avenue and went to get a slice of pizza. He was drunk, but he hadn't realized how drunk he was until he came inside the bright lights of the pizza place. He was so drunk that he was more drunk than anything else. He'd seen the Midtown Tunnel up ahead of him and he knew that he had to put something in his stomach right away. He hadn't wanted to eat much at dinner, and that had been a long time ago, and by the time he saw the Tunnel up ahead of him he was so cocaine-anxious that he could barely manage to open his mouth and ask Angie to ask the driver could they stop for the pizza before they went to Queens. His voice cracked when he spoke, and it sounded loud in his ears, but he was talking, so quietly that Angie, sitting next to him, could barely hear him. He'd been pouring beer down on top of the coke for hours, since Angie and Lynn had picked him up at his hotel. The plan had been to go to the Halloween parade in the limo that Lynn had rented for the week she was staying in New York. was Angie's first trip to New York. Lynn had brought her as a birthday present.

They hadn't made hotel reservations and somehow the only room that they could find was a suite in the Hyatt above Grand Central Station. It was on a private floor. Lavish and ugly. It cost a little less than twenty-one hundred dollars a night. They had been in New York for four days and they had only left their room twice. Once to eat at a very bad Chinese restaurant that Peter, their limo driver, had recommended, and once to go to a Western Union office on Seventh, where Lynn had picked up an extra ten thousand dollars that her father had wired to her from California. Neither of the girls had any credit cards and the hotel had wanted both a large deposit and daily payment in cash. In four days, they had not only run through the twenty-five thousand dollars that Lynn had brought for them, they had run out of cocaine as well.

Lynn had called her father. She said would he mind driving down to L. A. and going over to Angie's. If he stopped by her place first, there was a key in the spoon drawer. The ten thousand was stuffed inside Angie's mattress, on the far side by the wall where Jim slept.

Her father said, "Who the fuck is Jim?"

Lynn was proud of her father, and seemed to like the effect that her stories about him had on her listeners. She would say, "Straights just don't understand." She would say, "There's a code with cons; there's honor. Hell, my dad did seven in S. Q. for breaking and entering, and he'll probably be with a guy, Carol, can get you anything hot. I mean stolen elephant if that's what you want. Now Carol, he don't know Angie from shit, and he'll take anything, don't even matter if it is nailed down. But he's with Ed, and my old man says someone's good people, no one would fuck with that, any more than they'd steal from another con. So Carol won't take shit from Angie's house. It's like mutual respect, you know?"

Another thing she would say, "My old man went in when I was six. That's where he met all the people he does business with. They set it up while he was still inside. Even had a guy come around to check in on me and my brother, Walker."

One time she had said, "It's the only kind of people I can be around, 'cause I really bother some people 'cause they just can't handle it that I'm like a criminal, right? So it's guys that have done time and rock-and-rollers. What do you think of Ray Toro?"

It seemed to Alex that Lynn never stopped talking long enough to take a breath. She was a short fireplug of a girl. She looked like she had been put together by someone who had used one of those "how to draw" books. A series of ovals assembled into a woman's body. Oval thighs, round hips, round breasts, round head. She wore her dirty blonde hair short. A greasy strand constantly in her face. She would pause in the middle of a sentence, wipe that strand back off her forehead, and then bend to take a big line of coke while Alex waited in dread for it to kick in, amping her non-stop monologue. She would always move through the same three subjects:

Ray Toro, the only guy in My Chemical Romance who mattered. You could keep the rest of them; they were all junkies anyway.

Cars. She would spout stats and compare engines in Cobras, old Chevies, chopped Camaros. It seemed that she had owned every street race vehicle ever souped.

Her father. She would go from the Camaro into a story about some super-charged Toronado her dad used to out-run the police, a packaged bag with a pound and a half of pure Bolivian coke inside it breaking open and spilling all over the back seat, the powder up in the air until she and the old man were buzzing so hard that all that they could see was a bright white light.

From the little he knew about Angie and a few things she'd told him about Lynn, Alex was fairly sure that Lynn's stories were true. It was just that, at some point, the onslaught became so intense that it didn't matter whether the stories had happened or not. He had always imagined that real life criminals were very mater-of-fact. Boring. He thought that part of their "code" would be the simple piece of advice that he'd been given once by a very non-criminal pothead in college."Never commit a misdemeanor with a felony in your pocket."It didn't seem all that savvy to him to soup up a car and crank it to ninety when you were running cocaine. Maybe that was because he was a "straight," and straights really never would understand.

He hadn't known that he would be in New York when Angie had told him that Lynn was taking her there. He'd run into her at the bar at Harvard and Stone; hadn't seen her in a couple of years and she'd wanted to know: was he still playing any music? She'd said that Lynn was taking her to New York, that it was her first time there. Angie was gorgeous. The kind of gorgeous that didn't seem real. Eurasian, with dark eyes that promised kindness and understanding and a comfortable self-confidence that only comes with a certain kind of beauty. She was a girl you fell in love with. Alex had wanted to impress her. Sound like a well-traveled guy. A guy with a lot going on. He told her about a good Haitian restaurant in Williamsburg and promised that Harlem wasn't really as scary as everyone said. Then he'd given her his friend Tony's phone number. The girls had called Tony as soon as they'd checked into their hotel. Tony had come over and they'd stayed up all night, snorting coke and drinking vodka that Lynn had ordered from room service by the bottle.

"She's an outlaw," Tony'd told Alex. It was two days after he'd met Lynn and Angie. Alex had come in the night before. It was six in the morning and they were walking back uptown to Alex's hotel from the Hyatt.

"I think she's gotten used to the effect she has on people," Alex said. "Probably couldn't tell the kids in school about her dad, or maybe she got teased. Now it's exciting to people. Crime is an adventure. You get to know somebody dangerous."

Tony said, "Crime's like being black; it's a happening thing right now. I mean taking drugs, that's an adventure for chicken shits. But real crime; it's a weird kind of status. I guess because you've got to be extremely brave to pull it off."

"Gets you into parties."

"So does being black. Let me tell you this idea I thought about the night before last, for a movie. You should probably be stoned on pot before you hear it, but you're gonna love it, I promise you. It's about this government test site, top secret, in the Arizona desert. The place is underground." They were walking west on 57th now, the wide street nearly empty at four in the morning. "Or do you not want to talk about movies right now? I mean you're here, this is like your comeback tour or some shit."

"Just here to write some songs."

"You fucked up your voice or something, right?"

"Or something."

"And now you're writing songs with a rock star. That's all right, even if he is kind of a poser. So Angie, did you ever hit that?"

"When I knew her she was dating this guy from Nashville. He was in the Kings of Leon."

They were still very coked out and drunk when they reached his hotel. Tony left him at the front door. He said, "Unless you're gonna get to fuck Angie, I'd stay away from those girls. You want to be in fighting trim when you sit down with Nick Forest. This is not the kind of situation you want to fuck up."

"I'm not going to fuck anything up."

Tony looked at him skeptically for a moment. "In the day," he said, finally, "you could party with the professionals. What I'm saying is, this is not the day."

Alex fell asleep quite easily, considering how much coke he'd taken. But he woke up less than two hours later, wide awake and not at all refreshed. He got up, showered, dressed, and gathered up his folder and the small notebook in which he'd been jotting down stray lyrics since he got on the plane at LAX. Then he went downstairs to have breakfast. He liked the notebooks. They fit nicely in a pocket and they felt solid in his hand. They were earth brown with a black binding. Three by seven. They made him think of novels written in pencil. He had found a half-dozen in a Woolworth's in Cleveland when he was still touring with the band. Filled one with the only poems he had ever written and probably would ever write and put the notebooks away in a drawer. When he'd gotten the call to come to New York, he'd packed the five remaining notebooks. He was glad that he'd brought them. He thought that they gave him a look that was both diligent and still definitely arty. A serious wordsmith. Alex was in New York to try to write the lyrics for Nick Forest's first solo album. They were going to have an early dinner tonight and then start writing the next day at Nick's place in Connecticut.

Alex wanted to look like someone whom Nick could trust to capture the lyrical vision that was to inform that album.

He had left for New York the morning after Nick Forest's manager had called, the manager'd said that Nick really liked the lyrics that Alex had sent, but he'd thought they'd do better in a room together, working on something new. Could Nick come to New York the next day? Maybe they could try to beat out a couple of hits.

Nick Forest was a very major star. The lead singer in a band that had had one of the longest and most successful careers of any American group. He was a big, handsome blond, thin-boned, and skinny. He had an incredible voice and an arrogant way about him that most people found charming.

There had been a long musical dead spot in the early twenty-first century that Nick Forest and his band, Forest Fire, had filled for Alex. He'd gone to see them three times at clubs in Los Angeles. There wasn't much music coming out then that wasn't studied, and Nick was the one guy who didn't seem to care if anyone was watching. There was a short time when they'd been the band that Alex had put on while he was in the shower, the window open, and the music hitting like the warm breeze on his wet face. Then Nick and the band had started to think about what they were doing. His singing had kept improving, but he was using his chops to gloss over his increasingly weak lyrics. And then yet another neo punk explosion had brought rock and roll back and Alex had forgotten all about Nick and his group.

It seemed that a lot of other people had forgotten about them too. They staggered through a couple of disastrous albums until they were all but forgotten, and then they pulled their masterstroke. They came back with shorter hair, a striking T-shirt-and-jeans look, and an unbroken string of simple, well-arranged songs that were all phenomenal hits.

For college kids trying to stay musically hip without having to listen to anything that might make them think too hard, Forest Fire was the perfect band.

Alex didn't like their new music at all, partly because Nick's lyrics didn't touch him anywhere and partly because he had started to find Nick's onstage arrogance more offensive than charming. Now, about to work with Nick, Alex thought that he could go either way, remembering the music that had been an oasis of cool in the desert of the last decade, or picturing the poser who was not quite as cute as he thought that he was. Probably, Alex knew, he would go both ways at once. He would talk himself into liking Nick because he was working with him and he would look for any little hypocrisy that he could report back to his friends. He had already downloaded the band's last two albums, and he knew that pretty soon he would start to think that maybe some of the songs weren't as bad as he'd first thought.

That night at dinner with Nick and his managers, Alex was much more nervous than he had expected to be. Of course, he had only slept the two hours, and that didn't help. He knew that he was talking too loud and too fast, that he was trying too hard to impress Nick with a review of the sort of hip information he remembered reading that the guy liked. Druid myths. Some new book about the Hellfire Club's exploits in 18th-century London. He was embarrassed all the while that he was talking but he couldn't make himself stop. Nick was a part of the real world of rock and roll, and Alex simply hadn't realized how badly he would want the man to like him. He'd even pulled one of the notebooks out and written down some offhand remark of Nick's. "That could be a good chorus," he said when he was sure that Nick had seen the notebook.

On the way back to his hotel after dinner, he got a text from Angie. She and Lynn wanted to go and see the Halloween parade. Did he want to come with them? They'd pick him up. What he needed was to go to sleep. Nick's manager was sending a car for him at ten in the morning to take him out to Connecticut. Before he'd left the restaurant, the manager had taken him aside. "Back a couple of years ago when you were here recording for us, I know you could get a little heavy into it," he said, touching his nose. "Used to buy from Anthony and them. That's not hard to understand. What I want is for you to take it easy tonight. Nick'll have a little weed, you need something once you're writing, but I want you sharp. We're done with all that, yes?"

And now it was three in the morning and he was eating pizza to try to take the edge off an eight ball of Lynn's cocaine before they drove to some guy's house in Jamaica, Queens, who was a friend of Peter, the driver, and could get Lynn another ounce.

He was getting back in the car, wiping pizza grease onto his jeans, when Lynn's phone gave out a text tone. "Daddy," she said to her phone. Then she looked at Peter. "What's the address in Queens? My dad just landed. I'm gonna have him meet us."

"I really ought to be getting back," Alex said. "I've got this writing session tomorrow."

"Nick Forest," Lynn said, "is the shit. I know a girl who fucked him once, though she said he had a little dick."

"Can you drop me back at my hotel?" Alex asked, getting in the car.

"We'll just run through the tunnel first, pick up the blow. We'll have you back in an hour."

That was the moment for Alex to say no thanks. He should have turned, walked up the street, and caught a cab. He would have been back at his hotel in twenty minutes.

Alex had known Nick Forest slightly for almost ten years. Nick had come to a wedding reception once where Alex was playing in the band. They both knew the groom and they were introduced. They had several other friends in common.

A few years later, Nick's managers had been interested in signing a band that Alex had been playing bass with. They had flown the band to New York to do some demos.

Alex had spent several months in New York recording with that band. He had seen Nick a few times while he was there, but there were always a lot of people around and they had never really had a conversation. There is a sort of Sun King system that functions for famous people. They are always kept at the center of a very specific world, and there are always people who orbit around them, reflecting back at them their glorious light.

Alex had seen the small-time versions of these orbiters when he had toured; in clubs where the local hotshot band was opening for the group that he had been touring with, the same group that the managers brought to New York to record. A local scene of girls and hangers on and out, spinning around these tiny, local suns. He had seen them in record company offices and he'd seen them backstage at concerts. More than anything else, he hated to hear them talk about whatever their star's current project was. He hated to hear them use the word "we."It was fame by association and it was something he had thought about it a lot. Why was it that saying you worked for Nick Forest meant more than saying you had a secure, steady job at an accounting firm? The Nick

Forest job could get you into nightclubs. It could get you laid. That made sense. But if it made you think more of yourself, that made no sense at all.

When you went out with Nick, it was those people who made it seem like this was the only world that there was, and it made Alex feel flattered to be a part of something that he had always thought of as corrupt and lame. Alex was enjoying himself, and that, after a while, was what began to bother him. He knew better. He knew about second-hand fame. It was just that he wanted his own version of what Nick had so badly that he couldn't tear himself back.

When the demos had been finished, Alex had come back to Los Angeles. The managers had been unable to get the band signed. Alex had left the band and gone back to working on his own music. He'd put together a band and done some recording of his own songs. None of that had worked out either.

He'd been knocking around L. A., working at Amoeba, selling used copies of other people's records, when he'd gotten that call from Nick's manager. Nick was about to start working on a solo album. He'd always felt a connection to Alex and he was hoping Alex would want to write with him. Why didn't he send anything he had? Any fragments, anything you've finished. Any rags, any bones.

And there it all was. Alex had sent the lyrics, excited in spite of his knowing better. Whenever he'd run into anyone from the record business, anyone who'd walked out on one of his band's showcases, he'd let them know that he was sending Nick Forest lyrics for his solo album, that Nick and he would be getting together soon to work on the tunes. It was a sweet moment of fuck you, but it was a moment that could all blow up in his face. It was all up to Nick.

Coming back to New York, Alex wanted to remember this thing that he knew, that riding in the limo to the Staples with Chris Martin didn't make you anymore the star of the show than the guy back in the top of the 300s, so far away he couldn't tell which one Martin was without looking at the giant screen.

Alex was pretty sure that he knew what Nick Forest wanted. Rock and Roll had begun as poor people's music, a rebel yell. Nick Forest had become an industry. It is hard to be an industry and keep on yelling. It might be impossible. After eighteen years in the same band, after twenty top-ten singles, two Grammy awards, and the fourteenth-biggest-selling album of all time, Nick Forest wanted very badly to yell. He wanted to scream until his throat bled. Alex thought that was the way it was with Nick. When he'd gone through his lyrics, he'd picked out the angriest ones he could find.

Song lyrics were probably his favorite thing in all the world. A lyric had to be a perfect attack. You got in and then you got back out as quickly as you could, and as long as you didn't go in preaching, you always came back with something learned. His lyrics were always ahead of him. He'd sing about things he hadn't lived yet, things that he would only understand years later. He'd quoted himself more than once, thinking of some lyric which fit perfectly in a situation, and wondering for hours what Radiohead song he was quoting, before remembering that it was some throw-away line from a tune his band had written so that they could do three sets in bars without repeating too many songs.

Looking back through all his lyrics as he got them ready to send to Nick, going back over songs he hadn't sung in years, and some he'd never sung at all, he was satisfied that, for him anyway, the lyrics did what his favorite lyrics by other people did: put into words things you'd always thought, but had never been able to say. His criticism of his own work was scathing. He believed he had to see everything at its absolute worst, see all the most awful reasons why, and if it survived that grim assault, only then would he have the thing truly for his own. He had been a good bass player, a mediocre guitar player, and a two-finger pianist. His songs only became complete for him in a recording studio or on a stage. He loved that moment when the band snapped in, everybody finding their own way into the song. He wasn't good with arrangements. He'd get some simple ideas; let the other guys do whatever they thought worked. Say once in awhile if he didn't like it. Some people could do it all themselves, go from song to record in their own living room. He couldn't do that at all. And so he looked at all these words on paper with melodies that only existed, half-formed, in his head. And it seemed like such a waste.

He'd thought about trying to write something new, something for Nick. He'd tried to remember lyrics to any of Nick's big songs. They were all love songs, he thought. A few of them had girls' names in them. He got as far as "Girl U don't... U don't go breaking a heart like that," hearing it with a melody that sounded like one of Nick's. It was terminally dumb. He'd have to download more of Nick's songs. Maybe he shouldn't. If the guy wanted his sort of lyrics, he'd write them himself. That was when he'd realized that Nick would want to scream and had started to look for his angriest lyrics. He picked through his piles of papers and took out all his favorites. The best one was a finished song. One he'd recorded with his band. He was proud of it, both the melody and the words. He wrote little descriptive notes to Nick along with each set of lyrics. On the ones to the finished song he was so proud of he wrote, "I really like this lyric, but I'm stuck with a ditsy melody. Help me." It had become very important to him to get a song onto Nick's new record.

He'd never tried the kind of songs Nick wrote. Nick's songs now were rich men's tunes. Composed in a studio while they were recorded. Start with a bit of an idea, a chord progression or a few bars of melody; lay down a beat and some keyboards. The lyrics seemed like almost an after-thought. With Alex, the lyrics almost always came first, or poured out together with a simple melody. But it was the lyrics that pulled at him. Maybe, he had often thought, because he wasn't really much of a musician. But it was what he loved. He loved to stand at a microphone and let the words pour out of him. Words again, but they had to be sung. The melody mattered. But to be able to stand in front of people, strip yourself down. He could confess things in a song that he wouldn't even say to himself. It was like the talky way you'd get drunk sometimes, only it was truer than that.

The band that Alex had put together when he came back from recording in New York had done Alex's songs and a few well-chosen covers. But there wasn't much of a music business anymore—you were either a star of the magnitude of Nick Forest or you just put your songs up online and hoped for a viral miracle. Nothing like that had been happening for Alex and his band. The songs were raw, full of a frustration and pain that couldn't find a place in the Brooklyn banjo world of the eastside rock scene. Still, they had begun to develop a local following and had done several club tours of California and the southwest, and gotten a couple of great write-ups on a few of the live music blogs and in the Weekly. Almost in spite of themselves, a couple of guys from what was left of the record business had started to sniff around. Alex and the drummer had set up showcases at the Echo and The Hotel Cafe. It was one last shot and they had decided to take it.

Alex had been hoarse for several months. He'd been angry when they played, and he'd screamed through the sets. He had gotten to the point where he could lose his voice after every show.

When he'd gone to a doctor, he'd been told not to talk for six months. The doctor had had gold records on his walls. He was physician to the stars. He'd told Alex he'd better forget about singing for at least a year. Singing would leave him, the doctor had said with a "with it" smile, talking like Satchmo for the rest of his life.

It had taken Alex several days to realize that a doctor with a sense of humor so bad he thought, "Sing like Satchmo" was clever had told him that he was never going to be able to do the one thing he loved most in the world.

There is some iPhone footage from around that time. It was made a couple of weeks before Alex went to see the doctor. The band was playing a club date in Phoenix, what was going to be one of their last shows. Alex, singing, is a man ruining an already severely damaged piece of equipment. Listening to him on the phone footage, even with its poor quality, you hear his voice literally tearing, ripping, and ultimately shredding itself beyond all repair.

At their rehearsal the night before the first showcase, Alex had told the other guys in the band that he wanted to do a loud, thrashing version of the Dylan song, "It's All Right, Ma, I'm Only Bleeding." The version he'd wanted to do was Motorhead fast, and he'd put it in a key so high that he had to strain to hit the notes, which he had said would give their version some added desperation. The chords had been easy. He'd shown them all the way he wanted the riff, against which he was going to sing to go. Then they had dived in. On the fourth verse, he'd felt something tear in his throat. He'd finished the song and then asked to do it again. The drummer had told him that maybe he ought to take a break, not blow his voice out before the show. "This is fucking important," he'd said. "You can't fuck it up on some old song." Alex had told him to shut the fuck up; they needed to practice the song until they got it tight. He had never screamed that much in his life. It was all that he wanted to do.

This time, though, it had been obvious by the second verse of the song that Alex's voice was gone. The band stopped and the drummer called the rehearsal. The next morning, they'd canceled both of the showcases. There had been nothing left of Alex's voice but a hoarse whisper and a three-note range. The band had broken up, and Alex had gotten the job at Amoeba. There was something he'd written in a song a few years before that. "If you lose your legs, then you can't walk. If you can't walk, you can't fall down." What he'd felt, more than disappointment or frustration, was a great sense of relief.

When he'd gotten the text from Angie, it had seemed so perfect. He was there, in New York, nice hotel, gonna write some songs with a hit maker, and the hottest girl he'd known in his band days, a girl who'd been unapproachably perfect back then, was in town and wanted to see him. "Live the fucking life," he told himself. "Live the fucking life"

So then it was three in the morning and he was going to Queens in a limo with Angie and the "outlaw" Lynn and her criminal father was going to meet them at a coke dealer's house and even if Alex could get it up after all the coke, even if Angie would have any interest in coming up to his room, it would be probably five in the morning, and he would need at least a shower and some eggs to separate the day to come from tonight. He was fucked. Then he felt Angie's hand on his leg. "I hope this doesn't hang you up too much," she said. "Lynn is always an adventure."

It was a two-story clapboard house on a corner. The yard was tidy, but the yards of the other houses on the block had gone to weeds. Peter, the driver, parked and said that he would go in first. He'd called the guy, and he had what they wanted, but he didn't want a bunch of people coming into his house at three in the morning. Lynn gave him some money, because, as she said, what was he going to do? They had his car. When Peter heard that, he took his keys.

"Can't even play the radio," Lynn said. She looked out the window at the weeds in the yard across the street. "This neighborhood, man, it's bleak."

Angie leaned over, kissed Alex on the cheek. "You're worrying, aren't you? You won't have the ideas for the songs. You'll be too fried."

"I'll give you a couple of grams," Lynn said. "You'll be fine."

"It's just kind of a big deal for me," Alex said, more to himself than to the girls.

"You shouldn't have come out then," Lynn said. "I always say, the only decision you make is the decision to go out."

Then the driver's door opened. It wasn't Peter who got in. It was a middle-aged guy. Gray hair, a pockmarked face. He was holding a briefcase. "Hi, honey," he said to Lynn. "Give your old man a kiss and let's take this baby for a spin." He was holding Peter's keys. There was what looked like blood on his hand. He smiled.

The first gunshot shattered the rear window of the limo just as Lynn's father pulled away from the curb. Angie ducked, throwing herself into Alex' lap. He couldn't bend over now. She was in his way. There was broken glass in his hair and some of it had cut his neck. The second shot whizzed past his ear and lodged in the navigation controls. "Motherfucker!" Lynn's father shouted. "Now how the fuck do we find the tunnel?"

He swung the limo blindly around a corner, sideswiping half a dozen parked cars. He took another corner so fast that he went up on the curb and sent a trashcan flying, and they were on a broad boulevard. The street was wet and it re-flected the halogen glow of the streetlights. There were a few lights on in the closed businesses on either side of the street. Up the street was a McDonald's, and the morning shift was already inside.

"Give them five minutes to lick their wounds, get a car." Lynn's father said, as if doing a math problem. He turned to Lynn. "Call it in. You heard gunshots. You remember the ad-dress? If the cops get there soon, it'll buy us more time."

He reached down, opened the briefcase. It was full of cocaine. Pounds and pounds of cocaine. "Oh, daddy!" Lynn said. "Jackpot." Lynn's father turned to the back seat now, still driving. "Angie," he said. "Nice to see you." Then to Alex. "I'm Ed. You ever see so much fucking cocaine?"

They parked the limo in an alleyway off the wide street, which Lynn's father, Ed, said was Jamaica Avenue. What was funny, he said, the guys he took off for the cocaine, they were Jamaican and they lived in Jamaica, Queens. "You the guy is writing songs with Nick Forest?" he asked Alex. "Lynn said she was hanging out with a guy who knew a rock star." He opened the briefcase, took out one of the baggies of cocaine. He scooped a handful out with four fingers, snorted what must have been more than a gram, held the rest out. The blood on his hands, and it definitely was blood, had dried.

Lynn had long fingernails, and she scooped some coke up for herself, then for Angie, and then for Alex.

Alex didn't want any of the cocaine, but he thought that if he didn't take any Ed would start in on that and so, when Lynn reached him with her fingernail full of coke, he snorted. Ed licked the rest of the coke off of his fingers, put the bag back into the briefcase.

"Let's go find the train," he said. "Leave Jamaica to the fucking Jamaicans." Then he said, "Shit." And then he pulled out a handgun.

"Stay here," he said. "It's that fucking other guy from the house."

"What other guy, Daddy?" Lynn asked.

"Drug dealers, you know. They always got a friend. I take him out, the dealer I mean, and I do the driver when he comes in. I'm throwing the shit in the briefcase; this Rasta nigger in his underwear comes from some other room. The guy is crying like a bitch and then he comes at me with a kitchen knife. I thought I killed that motherfucker too, but I guess I missed. Gotta fix that shit."

He got out of the car and started at a run up the alley. The three of them sat there. At first, no one spoke, and then Angie said, "Shit, Alex," then they sat for a while longer, and then Ed came back.

"Was a different Rasta nigger," he said. "Man I'd never seen, just out walking it off. Guess I did drop the other one. "He grinned. There was coke caked all around his nose and now he brought a finger up, wiped it away, and rubbed the residue on his gums. "Let's go find the train."

As they were walking up the alley, Ed said to Alex, "Lynn said you used to play in some bands."

Alex nodded and Ed broke into a broad, crazy smile.

"Rock and Roll!" he screamed. "Rock and Roll!"

They were almost back to the street now, at four in the morning, in a really bad part of New York. The guy was carrying a briefcase full of cocaine and there was a stolen limo with the rear window shot out, and this guy, dried blood all over him, was screaming, "Rock and roll," at the top of his lungs. Then a plane landing at JFK roared overhead and there was no way Ed could shout over that.

It was almost ten in the morning when they got through the Park and pulled up by his hotel. They took the train in from Queens, and then they went to a midtown coffee shop. Ed told Lynn and Angie they would have to leave their shit at the Hyatt; if they went back to their suite there might be trouble since that was where Peter had picked them up. Then Ed called another car company, got them picked up. They would drive around for a while and then go back to Kennedy, catch the evening American flight back to L. A.

"You hang out with all these rock stars and etcetera, you want to keep a pound or two of this shit, sell it for me?" Ed asked Alex. "That's all right," he said before Alex could answer. He sounded contemptuous, as if Alex had already started to make excuses. "I got my people in L. A. Why don't we just drop you off back at your hotel?"

As they pulled up onto Central Park West, Angie leaned over to kiss Alex. "Call me when you're back in L. A.," she said. "I hope you write a hit song."

They were across from the hotel, by the 63rd street entrance to the Park. Alex got out and stood there as the car drove off. He saw Nick's driver leaning against his car outside the hotel. He was on his phone. Then Alex's cell buzzed a text. "Still downstairs. I can wait another five minutes." He saw that he had four other texts from the driver. With everything they'd been doing, he hadn't noticed them as they had come in.

He could go across the street, ask the driver to wait. He could run upstairs, take a quick shower and grab his notebooks. He could sleep a little in the car on the way to Connecticut if he could cut through the fading coke high. But for what? To say he wrote a song with Nick Forest? What would that be? "Girl U can't go breaking a heart." Fuck that. He would wait across the street here until he saw Nick's car drive off. Then he would go upstairs, take a long shower, and see what was on TV if he couldn't sleep.

THE CURE
DOUG WALLACE

"Give me your hand," said Abuelo as he took Carlos by the arm and lifted him from the platform into the first class cabin of the speedrail car. Carlos was only slightly embarrassed that Abuelo hadn't let him climb into the train on his own. After all, he was nine. But there was comfort in feeling his grandfather's strength, so he didn't fuss. He wondered whether he would still be so strong at one hundred and eighty.

The afternoon's rain that had washed the asphalt clean sent steam wafting up from the ground, causing Carlos' shirt to cling uncomfortably to his back. But the cabin was cool and the seat cushions comfortable. Best of all, since his parents were back in coach, he would have the entire three-hour ride from Minneapolis to Miami to be alone with Abuelo.

A uniformed woman with a big smile and pretty blue eyes strode down the aisle, stopping at each row, asking the passengers for tickets to scan. When she got to Abuelo, she held out her hand expectantly. Her silver fingernails and delicate-looking hands drew Carlos' attention. Abuelo smiled a warm smile.

"Today is my Passing, and my grandson here is my Chosen."

Two free first class tickets on the speedrail for anyone on their Passing Day. One for the person passing, and one for the person chosen to be with them at the end. The woman smiled cordially and glanced sideways at Carlos. He'd seen that look before and knew that as long as he was with Abuelo, it wouldn't be the last. They said Abuelo was the most famous biotech engineer in the world. More often than not people recognized him. Carlos was proud to be his grandson. A hundred and twenty years ago, Abuelo had invented the nanites that made diseases go away. He had donated the cure so that rich and poor alike would have it. That was why they had given him the Nobel Prize.

Abuelo leaned forward and tugged at Carlos's seatbelt to ensure it fit snugly around his waist. A smile crept across his craggy face as he winked. Carlos smiled back. He knew what Abuelo's Passing meant, but still he could not bring himself to feel happy. It was supposed to be the celebration of a long and healthy life. Carlos wondered whether Abuelo was celebrating. How could he be? How could anyone be happy to die? Yet somehow Carlos could sense that Abuelo was at peace.

"Aren't you going to ask me about your inheritance, Carlito? I promised I'd give you more clues on the ride to Miami."

Abuelo had insisted on going to a funeral home in Miami so he could be laid to rest next to his mother. He was born in Cuba, but when he was still very young, Abuelo's family had immigrated to the United States. The land of freedom. The land of laws. Laws that now required Abuelo, having reached the appointed age, to die. They called it the Passing. But Carlos knew it was a nice way of saying murder. Of hiding what they were really doing to Abuelo. Why did the law even apply to him anyway? If anyone deserved special treatment, it was Abuelo. Hadn't he given enough to the world? He was too famous, too important to die. Carlos held back a tear. He would give away a thousand inheritances if it meant Abuelo didn't have to die.

"My friend Sumi was a Chosen, too. Her grandpa gave her a lot of money for her inheritance. Are you going to give me money?"

Carlos knew it wouldn't be money. Despite his fame, Abuelo wasn't rich. He had already given most of his wealth away to charities, and what little he had left wouldn't amount to much of an inheritance. Abuelo shook his head.

"Carlito, you can do better than that. Guess again."

The speedrail train had reached cruising speed by now. Carlos watched as the slums, stacked higher than some older skyscrapers, streaked by his window. They seemed to go on for miles. He remembered what Abuelo had told him before, that the population explosion had been his fault. Because of his nanites.

"Well, you did bring me a batch of your famous homemade chocolate chip cookies. And I ate every last one just like you said to."

Abuelo smiled warmly and nodded, and the twinkle in his eye appeared again. "Oh no, Carlito, your inheritance is better than my famous cookies." He looked thoughtful. "But I am pleased you liked them."

Just as soon as the urban sprawl of Minneapolis ended, the slums of Chicago seemed to begin. The scene was the same: houses crookedly stacked up to the sky like old-fashioned building blocks. And it was the same with Indianapolis,

Chattanooga, Atlanta, and Jacksonville, an endless stream of people and places with people. At each stop, hundreds of passengers boarded or got off the train.

Carlos tried to imagine what it had been like before, when Abuelo was his age. Real farms with fields. Vast forests. A night sky uncluttered by orbital condominiums. "It's a shame," Abuelo had said once, "We are spreading like a disease, infecting the planet. Earth won't survive much longer if mankind doesn't change." Carlos had always thought it a strange thing to say, but seeing all the people crammed together in the towering slum-shacks made him understand, if only a little more.

After a half hour of watching out the window, wondering of Abuelo and things of the past, Carlos's thoughts were brought back to the present by his increasing discomfort. He was growing hot and tugged at the collar of his shirt. He knew it loosened somehow but struggled to get it open. Abuelo reached over to help him. Sweat trickled down Carlos' temples.

"Are you as hot as I am?" he managed to ask Abuelo, who placed his index finger to his lips in the sign for quiet.

"It must be the sun. We're in Florida now. They don't call it the Sunshine State for nothing," he said.

But Carlos knew there was more to it than that. Nobody else in the First Class cabin seemed to be sweating. And his head was starting to hurt with a pounding like a drum. He'd never felt quite like it. Before long, he was asleep.

When Abuelo woke him up, Carlos was freezing. Had they turned down the temperature in the cabin? The train was no longer moving, and the doors were open. Hot and humid air seemed to slap Carlos in the face as he and Abuelo stepped onto the platform. Mother and Father were there, having gotten off back in coach and battled their way through the throngs of people at the train station to the doors of the First Class lounge.

Abuelo turned to face Carlos, placing his hands on his grandson's shoulders. He knelt down so his and Carlos's eyes were on the same level. Abuelo appeared to be unbothered by the pressing crowd that seemed to flow around them like water around a boulder in a stream.

"Carlito," he said. Tears had replaced the normal twinkle in his eyes. "I need to tell you what your inheritance is, but you must keep it a secret. Do you promise?"

Carlos turned his head and buried his face in the bend of his arm as he endured a coughing fit. The dust from the platform must be bothering him more than he originally thought.

"I promise, Abuelo." He was feeling a little weak in his knees, and was suddenly aware of his aching body. Despite that, he seemed to tremble with excitement at the thought of what his Grandfather was leaving him as his inheritance.

Abuelo leaned in and whispered in Carlos' ear. His excitement faded to confusion. Abuelo hugged Carlos one last time and turned to the lift that would take them all to street level. Carlos's Mother motioned to follow them as they joined Abuelo. Carlos felt light-headed but managed to reach the elevator in spite of his dizziness.

What was wrong with him? Why was he feeling this way? And why had Abuelo given him such a strange inheritance? Of what worth were whispered words? Carlos would keep the secret as he'd promised, but could not wait to find out what being patient zero meant.

ACKNOWLEDGEMENTS

In addition to you dear reader, we'd also like to thank a few other folks who helped with the production of this book.

Faith Kretch, our ruler of all things social media. Faith also did quite a bit of reading from the submission pile and is generally just about as helpful as one person can be.

Nikita Hernandez appeared in Affinity with "Sexting is Such a Bad Habit", we liked her perspective so much we asked her to help us with our story selection. Her comments are always well thought out and were most helpful in whittling down the huge pile of submissions.

We met Rebecca Harrelson last year when Yes! Weekly wrote a piece about us. One conversation led to another and we knew we'd found a lifelong friend. Rebecca is always good for an opinion and her enthusiasm is infectious. She too was helpful in picking stories for this anthology.

Nancy Slagle brought some much needed outside perspective to the editing process. She shares our values when it comes to preserving the intent of the author, and we appreciate her patience and thoughtfulness.

Bradley Powell makes Matt's cover visions work. He's also very patient and has yet to yell at me for standing over his desk like a vulture.

We'd also like to thank all of the writers in Exhibits, as well as every other writer we've published, whether in print or online. It's you that inspire us to keep working even when the candle has burned right on through the middle.

And finally, Ali and Caroline... thank you for continuing to roll with the madness. Your love and encouragement keeps everything together; we couldn't do it without you.

ABOUT THE AUTHORS

Leah Mueller is an independent writer from Tacoma, Washington. She is the author of one chapbook, "Queen of Dorksville", and two full-length books, "Allergic to Everything" and "The Underside of the Snake." Her work has been published or is forthcoming in Blunderbuss, Memoryhouse, Atticus Review, Thank You For Swallowing, Sadie Girl Press, Origins Journal, Silver Birch Press, Cultured Vultures, Quail Bell, and many others. She was a featured poet at the 2015 New York Poetry Festival, and a runner-up in the 2012 Wergle Flomp Humor Poetry contest.

Douglas W. Milliken is the author of the novel *To Sleep as Animals* and several chapbooks, most recently the collection *Cream River* and the forthcoming pocket-sized edition *One Thousand Owls Behind Your Chest*. His stories have been honored by the Maine Literary Awards, the Pushcart Prize anthology, and *Glimmer Train Stories*, and have been published in *Slice*, the *Collagist*, and the *Believer*, among others. "Dummy" originally appeared in the *Manchester Review* and was written as part of a fellowship with the I-Park Foundation.www.douglaswmilliken.com

Mark Blickley lives and works in New York City and is a widely published author of fiction, nonfiction, poetry and drama. His most recent book is the story collection "Sacred Misfits" (Red Hen Press) and his drama, "The Milkman's Sister," premieres November 5th at NYC's 13th Street Repertory Theater. A text based art collaboration with photographer Amy Bassin, "Dream Streams," was recently published in "Columbia: A Journal of Literature and Art." He is a proud member of the Dramatists Guild and PEN American Center.

Mike Sherer–A movie made from my screenplay 'Hamal_18' was produced and released direct to DVD. It is available to purchase at Amazon or to rent at Netflix. My mystery/fantasy novel 'A Cold Dish' was published by James Ward Kirk Fiction and is available at Amazon in paperback and digital format. I am serializing my science fiction/fantasy novel 'Uncertain Cat' at channillo.com. I have published five short stories and a novella. I post my blog 'flanging' at mikesherer.wordpress.com

Doug Wallace is a father of four kids who love the "mouth stories" he tells them each night before going to bed. After publishing his first short story in the creative section of a graduate student journal in college, he took a fifteen year break to focus on his career in the IT security field, where he currently works to pay the bills. After being selected for a summer intensive with Orson Scott Card, Doug has written over twenty scifi short stories and is working on a number of scifi/fantasy book projects. His work can be found in anthologies by Centum Press (vol. 2 and 3), Just a Minor Malfunction (JAMM), and in online literary journals such as Metamorphose and Inside the Bell Jar. He loves technology, history, and writing about his observations of what makes people tick. He frequently posts select short stories on his website–https://jamesdouglaswallace.com/

George Losey–Blame the whiskey. I'm just an innocent by-stander after 5 o'clock.

Craig Hartglass is a native of New England. His stories have appeared in One Story, The Sun, The Saint Ann's Review, and most recently, The Malahat Review.

Les Bohem was a small part of the great Los Angeles music scare of the 1980s, both with his own band, Gleaming Spires, and as a member of the band, Sparks. Somehow that evolved into a career writing for the movies and television and before he knew how it had happened, he'd written some movies and TV shows including Twenty Bucks, Daylight, Dante's Peak, The Alamo and the mini-series, Taken which he wrote and executive produced with Steven Spielberg. and for which he won an Emmy award. He's had songs recorded by Emmylou Harris, Randy Travis, Freddy Fender, Steve Gillette, Johnette Napolitano (of Concrete Blonde), and Alvin (of the Chipmunks. His short novel, Flight 505, was published last year by UpperRubberBoot . Right now, he's producing his series, Shut Eye, starring Jeffrey Donovan, KaDee Strickland, Angus Sampson and Isabella Rossellini for Hulu. His new album, "Moving to Duarte," will be out in November.

David Crouse is an award-winning short story writer and teacher. His collection of short fiction, Copy Cats, received the Flannery O'Connor Award for Short Fiction in 2005 and was nominated for the Pen-Faulkner the following year. A second collection, The Man Back There, was published in 2008 by Sarabande Books and was awarded the Mary Mc-Carthy Prize in Short Fiction. His stories have appeared in some of the country's most well regarded journals, including Prairie Schooner, TriQuarterly, The Greensboro Review, The Southern Review, Chelsea, Quarterly West, and The Beloit Fiction Journal. His comic book writing has been anthologized in The Darkhorse Book of the Dead, published by Darkhorse Comics.

Victoria Griffin–After graduating from the English and softball programs at Campbell University, Victoria returned to East Tennessee where she works as a freelance editor. She is currently an editing mentor in the Pitch to Publication competition, and her short fiction has appeared in *NonBinary Review, A Journey of Words,* and *Incandescent Mind,* among other publications. When she's not writing or editing, she spends her time lifting weights and baking semi-healthy desserts. Find her at www.VictoriaGriffin.net.

Emily Auman is in her early twenties. Her greatest past times almost exclusively involve alcohol and poorly written television shows from the early 90's. She resides in the foothills of North Carolina and firmly believes the term "foothills" is a weird one. Follow her on emilywrites.net.

Andrew White has a degree in Psychology and has written extensively on drug addiction. The "Gun Show Loophole" is his first published work.

67 Press is a literary publishing collective founded to give fringe authors a vehicle to be heard. Our goal is finding talented people on the edge of society with something to say, but who don't fit into a neat little box for mainstream publishers. We find talent and help that talent work within their vision to create a finished product. We do all the things that other publishers do, but we do it with the author in mind, the bottom line or focus groups. We would never tell an author a book doesn't fit into a specific genre, it's too audacious, or "We just don't think it will sell." We believe great stories and great writing transcend subject matter and audience.

If we sound like a publisher you want to work with, please contact us. We'd love to hear from you:

http://67press.com/contact-67-press/